SMOLDER
A NOVELLA

WRITTEN BY
MICHAEL R. GOODWIN

Copyright © 2021 by Michael R. Goodwin

All rights reserved.

This is a work of fiction. Names, characters, businesses, places, events, locales, and incidents are either the products of the author's imagination or used in a fictitious manner. Any resemblance to actual persons, living or dead, or actual events is purely coincidental.

This book or any portion thereof may not be reproduced or used in any manner whatsoever without express written permission except for the use of brief quotations in a book review.

www.michaelrgoodwin.com

For my wife, Jessica –

*Thank you for being supportive of my writing,
even when it creeps you out.*

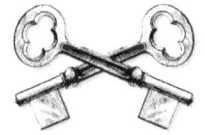

PROLOGUE

As the fourth largest city in Maine, Hamilton covers nearly 66 square miles. It is a diverse town, as most towns in central Maine are. Home to both farmland and densely packed urban blocks, it is a melting pot where the various demographics blend together whether they like it or not. The urban center of Hamilton is situated on the northeastern side where the Androscoggin River serves as the borderline between Hamilton and Lewiston.

On the southwestern half, suburbs and affluent neighborhoods reign supreme. Quiet streets and housing communities dotted with recently built schools give Hamilton the cleaner reputation over its twin sibling across the river. In reality, there are bad parts of Hamilton, too. They just manage to keep it cleaner, thanks in part to one special tool: Taxes. Property taxes in particular, and Hamilton's property taxes are among the highest statewide.

Despite that, the real estate market in Hamilton is always booming. That keeps land survey crews busy nearly the entire year-round, defining property lines every time a house goes under contract. Property taxes are assessed at a different (and much higher) rate in West Hamilton, and if a mortgage company is going to be on the hook for a large piece of land, they want to be sure about every square inch of it.

Such was the case for a large ranch property in West Hamilton that recently went under contract. The survey had to be completed before the loan could move forward. A survey company was hired and they sent out one of their younger surveyors for the job.

It was a warm spring day and he was glad to find that the ground was solid enough not to require his knee-high muck boots, yet he put them on anyway. Spring in Maine can be a crapshoot, and it is always best to be prepared. He shrugged on his backpack with all of his survey gear inside and went to find the first property marker. This was a large property to cover on foot and he wasn't paid by the hour.

The first three markers were pretty easy to find; two markers at the road and one at the northwestern corner, the furthest point away from the sprawling ranch. According to his map, the property made a sharp ninety-degree pivot and continued on for nearly a mile before doglegging back toward the house.

He sat down on a stump, pulled a water bottle out of his bag, and swallowed half of it in three gulps. Turned out he didn't need a sweatshirt after all, so he peeled it off and stuffed it into the top of his pack. He couldn't rest for long, as he had another property to map out after this one. Another sip of water and he was back on his feet, headed toward the fourth marker.

Somewhere along the way, he got lost.

He had never gotten turned around in the woods before. It was part of the reason why he became a surveyor in the first place; his natural sense of direction made his job pretty easy. He was so confident in his abilities to follow the map that he left his handheld GPS in his car, but his compass didn't seem to be working right. The needle kept spinning in lazy circles no matter what direction he faced. He checked his phone and saw there was no service, and he did his best not to panic.

It was approaching nightfall when the surveyor finally found the fourth property marker. It happened quite on accident. He had paused to put his sweatshirt back on, as the temperature in the woods had dropped, and there it was practically underfoot. He was overjoyed to have found it. It meant that he not only knew where he was on the map but based on the position of the setting sun in the sky, he knew what direction he needed to travel in to get back to his car.

It also meant he had surveyed enough of the property to call it quits. It was an industry secret among surveyors that when finding the markers proved to be a challenge, you called it quits after you found at least fifty percent of them. There was even an endearing quote that went along with it: *Fifty percent pays the rent.*

He checked his phone and, finding it had service, used his employer's app to log his job as complete, taking a moment to notate that the city of Hamilton's property map was accurate. It truthfully wasn't, but he was eight hours past caring. The job should have taken him around four hours to complete, and here he was, twelve hours later. He missed surveying the other property he had been scheduled for, and for an embarrassing reason.

He used the light from his phone to check his map so he knew which way to walk then tucked his phone back into his jeans pocket. Maybe it was his eyes readjusting to the dim light of the woods after looking at his bright phone screen, but the woods around him suddenly seemed immensely dark.

It was so dark, he could feel the weight of it on his skin.

Except it wasn't the darkness on his skin. It was something else, and it burned.

The surveyor screamed, the pain finally registering. He tried to brush off with his hands whatever was growing over his body, but it kept spreading. Thick and heavy and dark like a shadow.

He felt like his insides were boiling, and then an intense, white-hot flash filled his brain.

The surveyor collapsed to the ground, the bones in his legs and torso liquefying into jelly. The rest of him slowly capsized forward onto the oozing pile.

He saw a beetle scuttle by his right eye just before he felt something trickle down his nose. The vision in his left eye went black as that side of his face became covered in the blackness. He was dying, but that reality hadn't quite sunk in yet, and he was glad he had lost just one eye and not both. Having sight in one eye was better than no sight at all.

Fifty percent pays the . . .

The smolder finished spreading over the man, and when the Nothing was done with him, the dry earth took the rest.

1

It was dusk, but nighttime was quickly approaching. The sky was a gradient that brightened on the eastern horizon, glowing a dirty grey-white from the busy downtown hub of Hamilton.

Eric Roth sat on his back porch, watching the sky darken. His husky frame spilled out of his chair. The porch wrapped around the backside of his ranch-style home that sat on one hundred and forty acres of field and forest on the west side of Hamilton. His nearest neighbor was five miles away beyond an apple orchard. They were out far enough where they could not hear the sounds of Hamilton, but the glow in the sky couldn't be escaped.

"Look at the size of this place!" Monica remarked the day they moved in. "You could yell at the top of your lungs and no one would be close enough to hear it."

"That's kind of the point," Eric had said. "We finally have privacy."

As newlyweds, they had lived in their share of downtown apartments and suburban shoeboxes. They spent a decade living with neighbors on all sides, all while dreaming of one day owning a house where their nearest neighbor was more than a stone's throw away. When Eric finally got the promotion he had been promised for years, the extra income allowed them to make that dream a reality.

It took nearly a year of strict budgeting and penny-pinching on Eric's new salary (along with Monica's modest income as a pediatric nurse) to come up with a down payment. All they needed to do next was find the perfect house. When they saw the sprawling ranch on a massive parcel of land out in West Hamilton, they didn't look any further.

Three weeks after they moved in, Eric found out about his wife's affair. It was good there was no one around to hear them yell because there had been excessive amounts of yelling before she moved out, leaving him alone in his new (and very expensive) home.

    She had been sleeping with a guy at work, some asshole named Troy or Travis or Trent. Eric couldn't be bothered enough to remember. Turned out those shifts at the pediatric office that ran late weren't because they were short-staffed. The affair had been going on for more than a year, and Eric hated himself for not seeing it. It happened practically right under his nose, but he was distracted by his job, working extra hours to save up enough for the big down payment. He hated himself almost more than he hated his wife's (*ex-wife's*) lover.

    On the day Monica moved out, Eric heard a loud, rumbling exhaust on his normally quiet street. Eric went to the front door to investigate and saw a massive black truck lumbering up his driveway. Monica slid out of the passenger seat, climbing down awkwardly using the running boards. The truck was perched on ridiculously oversized tires, an aftermarket lift making the vehicle absurdly tall. It was a grotesque display of overcompensation, a suspicion confirmed when Monica's lover got out from behind the wheel.

    Monica pulled her brown hair back into a ponytail as she went over to Trevor or Trey or whatever, and despite wearing flats, she stood several inches taller. He wore designer jeans, pre-faded and pre-torn, and a tight MMA t-shirt. He was the stereotype douchebag, the kind of guy Monica embarrassingly confessed to having dated in college, except this one had a bald spot peeking out from his salon cut.

Even though he was only in his mid-thirties, Eric had been seeing gray in his hair for several years now. It never bothered him because he would take that over going bald any day.

Seeing him, knowing that his wife had thrown away a decade's worth of a good marriage for a man who probably liked to throw his woman around whenever he had one drink too many, Eric's anger over the situation evaporated. He had been stewing in his anger and self-doubt for weeks. What had he done to make his wife look for comfort in another man? Was he not good enough? Did he not do enough to make her happy? What did he lack that she required so badly that she would toss him to the curb so easily?

Eric was relieved to finally accept and understand that his wife's infidelity wasn't his fault after all. Monica had been tempted by this man who embodied her college youth and wasn't able to resist. He couldn't help but laugh as he opened his front door and stepped out onto the driveway to meet them.

"What's so funny, Eric?" Monica had asked.

"This is the guy? You're leaving me for this douchebag?"

Monica held her boyfriend back as he puffed up, shoulders pulling back to push out his fledgling pectorals. "Hey, who are you calling a—"

"Trent, don't. Just help me load up my boxes so we can get out of here," she begged quietly. Trent made a big display over the effort it took to calm himself down, but the redness in his face lingered. He was easily provoked, this one.

That didn't bode well for Monica, who was known to tease people relentlessly.

Monica led Trent by the elbow over to the garage door, which was already open in preparation for their arrival. A large gathering of boxes and a cluster of suitcases sat in the middle of the bay. Trent showed off by grabbing two of the biggest boxes at once. Eric silently wished that Trent would be struck with a hernia as he struggled to heave the boxes onto his tailgate.

Eric stood off to the side and watched as the two of them loaded everything up, with Trent's strongman bit making quick work of things despite the fact that he was visibly struggling.

There hadn't been much of Monica's things to pack up. Most of everything they owned was still in boxes as they had really just moved in, and whatever had been unpacked that she claimed was hers she packed in a wild fury the night of their worst shouting match. The night she walked out.

Whatever she had left behind after that night, Eric had packed up and moved out into the garage so she wouldn't come into the house. Eric was amazed at how easily the possessions gained through eleven years of marriage could be divided up once you got piss drunk and stopped caring.

Once Trent's truck was loaded up, Monica told him to get into the truck and wait for her. Trent locked eyes with Eric, staring him down before he reached over and slapped Monica on the ass.

"Hurry up," he said to her, not lowering his eyes.

Monica's face turned red. She tried to hide it by

looking at the ground as she walked up the driveway to where Eric stood. The garage door rattled down on its track. Trent's truck roared to life, the engine revving in his final pathetic display of overt masculinity.

"Look, Eric . . . I . . ." she began. She looked up, and Eric saw the words she had prepared freeze on their way out. "I never—"

Eric held up his hand, cutting her off.

"You made up your mind the second you slept with that guy. There's no coming back from that, and you know it."

Eric didn't want her apology any more than he wanted to have Trent's truck in his driveway. She had tried to apologize a few other times before, but hearing her express remorse now only served to make his stomach turn.

Eric wouldn't see Monica face to face again until they stood in front of a judge to settle their divorce.

That was eighteen months ago.

On that day, this house, the one that was supposed to be theirs, was now his.

In less than a week, it wouldn't even be that.

The bank was foreclosing since Eric couldn't afford the mortgage on his own, promotion be damned. It honestly would have been a tight fit even with both of them working full-time, but that plan hadn't exactly panned out. Monica moved out before he made their first payment, so he paid what he could. It was the snowflake that started the avalanche of debt and foreclosure, under which he was now deeply buried.

Eric made it as far as he could on his own, but it was an exercise in futility. What little money they had in savings was split in half by the judge, and because Eric made more than Monica, the judge granted her alimony. The mortgage was in Eric's name, a strategic decision that shouldn't have been used against him, but one that gave him sole responsibility for its repayment.

Between the alimony and a steep mortgage payment, it was only a matter of time.

That time was running out, and this was one of the last nights Eric would have in his house. Even though it was late October and temperatures were starting to dip below freezing, he was going to enjoy sitting on his goddamn porch while it was still his.

He shook his head, trying to clear his mind of the thoughts that would only push him further into the whiskey bottle that sat on the porch railing. He didn't want to think about Monica and Trent living together in their downtown Hamilton apartment. He didn't want to think about his home that will soon belong to the bank, its room's barren, nothing but beer in the fridge, and a sleeping bag and pillow in the living room.

It embarrassed him that he was living like a homeless person inside his spacious ranch home, but he sold everything he had to try to keep the place. He felt shameful, but at least no one could say he hadn't tried.

Eric stretched out his arm and grabbed the whiskey bottle off the railing, taking a strong pull before setting it back down. It burned and settled with warm turmoil in his belly.

"Fucking Monica," he said out loud, a phrase he had uttered to himself many times over the last year and a half.

The light staining the sky on the horizon was a reminder to him of where he was, and also where he wasn't going to be for much longer. It was where *she* was, she who had been the beginning of the end of so much.

The horizon glowed, and Eric became angry. It swelled up within his mind like the unraked leaves in the backyard when the wind blew. It was noisy and chaotic and seductive, the gears of his mind lubricated and liberated by the drugstore whiskey in his stomach.

He couldn't stand seeing the light on the horizon for a single second longer.

Eric stood up, grabbing the whiskey bottle by the neck on his way up. He turned toward the door that led into his house and stopped.

Going inside was a bad idea. His mind flashed, giving him premonitions of his fists going through the drywall, of him urinating on the plush carpet in the open concept living room. Eric decided against going inside, as the only silver lining to the foreclosure was the relocation incentive he was getting if he turned the property over in good condition. He couldn't afford to lose that money, no matter how drunk or pissed off he was. Some days, that money coming in was the only thing keeping him alive.

He took another pull off the bottle and turned to look at the backyard. In the almost-dark, he couldn't see very far, but he knew there was about fifty yards of turf ahead of the tree line. He remembered then that the woods (*his* woods, goddamn it) carried on for more than a hundred acres in the opposite direction of where the horizon was glowing.

That settled it. He recognized that it was a bad idea

to go for a walk in the woods alone, much less at night, much less while solidly drunk, but it was a better alternative to going inside. Staying put wasn't an option, so with unsteady feet and a nearly empty whiskey bottle in his hand, Eric stepped down off the porch.

It was cold outside, the tall grass crackling and crunching noisily under his feet. His back lawn hadn't been mowed in a while, as he sold his mower to help keep the lights on months ago. The grass had dried up and practically turned to hay, rasping against his jeans as he pushed through on the way to the woods.

Eric looked skyward as he walked, both unafraid and uncaring of whatever obstacles might be in his path. A thick scrim of clouds passed over, momentarily blotting out the stars and the moon. Without the light of the moon, Eric realized it was much closer to full dark than he had previously thought. He must have lost track of time when he was also lost in thought, but that didn't change his plans at all. As dark as it was around him, part of the night sky still belonged to the city lights of Hamilton, and he needed to put distance between himself and that glow.

He needed that distance more than anything, an all-consuming compulsion that felt like intense thirst.

He zigged and zagged across the lawn, his erratic trail marked in the tall, dead grass that lay flat in his wake. Looking up at the sky turned out to be a bad idea, the movement of the clouds making him dizzy. The alcohol swimming in his blood didn't help matters much, either. He peered into the void ahead of him, trying to make out where the lawn ended and the woods began.

Just as his eyes discerned the line of pines and firs

from the shadows, the tip of his shoe snagged on a gopher hole. His ankle twisted and down he went, tumbling to the ground in a graceless heap. The rough grass brushed coarsely across his face. Eric rolled onto his back, eyes closed, and laughed.

"That's going to hurt tomorrow," he said to himself.

Eric opened his eyes, staring up at the sky. The world was spinning faster than normal, ramping up like an amusement park ride. The motion he felt, combined with his shaken equilibrium, made the contents of his stomach reconsider their location. He squeezed his eyes shut, convincing his gorge to settle.

Several moments later, his stomach contents secured, Eric pushed himself off the ground. He rotated his ankle, testing it to determine if he was able to continue his walk. It was a little tight, but he thought it would loosen up as he went along. He took a few cautious steps and, finding the pain slight but bearable, decided to keep going.

He soon met the edge of his lawn, crossing over the threshold into the woods. It was much darker in the woods, the branches yawning upward and around him, blocking out what little light was offered up from the moon and stars behind the clouds.

It was the darkness inside the woods that made Eric first reconsider what he was doing. He had no flashlight (was too drunk to think to bring one before he left his house), and no cellphone (his service had gotten shut off just two days ago due to non-payment).

What if something were to happen?

What if he got lost?

Eric only briefly contemplated those questions

before he came to the conclusion that he quite simply didn't care.

It was just a walk in the woods to clear his head and make some breathing room.

He needed to create some space to put distance between where he was and the situation he was in. And there was that glow, the city lights from Hamilton. *Fucking Monica.* A gust of anger swelled up inside of him again, the pilot light that was his constant ire toward what had happened to him, toward what had become of his life, igniting the rolling blue flame that kept his body in motion.

He was oddly unafraid, despite the darkness in the woods being so thick he could barely see the whiskey bottle when he brought it to his lips. The whiskey definitely helped, emboldening his nerves and helping him forget about the coyote calls he had heard earlier in the evening.

Eric made it a few yards into the woods before the cloud cover dissipated and patches of moonlight filtered down through the canopy above, spattering the ground with dapples of grey light. It yielded enough visibility for Eric to see the ground in front of him, avoiding roots and low brush that he otherwise would have certainly tripped over.

He walked slowly, soaking in the sounds of the nocturnal creatures that were chirping and rustling around him in the shadows. A scratching scurry in the pine needles and leaves to his left, a snapping twig to his right, the subtle call of a bird Eric was sure he'd never heard before in his life. Taking efforts to tread carefully after tripping on the gopher hole, he stepped on a fallen branch that cracked easily and loudly under his weight.

An owl directly overhead loudly questioned Eric's

audacity in disturbing his hunt, taking to the air with a concussive burst of feathers. Eric ducked down but craned his neck upward to watch the owl fly off. He marveled at it, knowing he would have never known he had an owl in his woods if he had decided to stay home.

Home.

It wasn't going to be home much longer.

Eric's mind, the gears loose and slipping from inebriation, snagged on a splinter of a thought he tried to ignore. This sliver of reason offered him the possibility that the anger he felt toward his situation meant he still harbored feelings for the woman who brought an end to so many things.

Surely, that wasn't the case. How could you still feel that way for someone but at the same time, also hate them so vehemently?

This thought was a rabbit hole, one that a sober Eric would have known to steer clear of. The Eric that existed now was not capable of ignoring such a thing and grabbed hold of this notion with vigor.

He took a long pull from the bottle and walked deeper into the night.

2

Eric was not alone in the woods.

It observed him up close and from a great distance, seeing without the need for eyes, hearing without the need for ears. It felt every pine needle bend under the man's feet, felt the pull and release of every breath through the man's lungs. It could taste the bitter smokiness that mingled with the man's blood.

It was as old as the earth that the man tread upon and as young as newborn field mice, pink and naked and wriggling together for warmth.

It was everywhere, and in these woods, it was everything and it was Nothing.

It took refuge in the woods, hiding itself in the trees and in the undergrowth. It pooled on the ground, spreading out like a fog. It had a form that it rarely took, and on this night, it was shapeless and nearly invisible. It took a very keen eye to spot the Nothing. Most humans could not.

It felt the man walking through itself, oblivious to everything around him.

It rose from the ground, gathering the shadows around itself like a robe.

The Nothing stood, feeling foreign in its shape, towering over the tallest of the trees like a midnight sentinel. In the gloom, the Nothing opened its eyes. From underneath the hood of its shadowcloak draped over its head, two pools of white fire burned, blistering and flaring until simmering down into coals.

Through its own eyes, the Nothing could see through the canopy of trees as if the trees didn't exist. It watched as the man stepped over a cluster of withered ferns. The man talked to himself, but the Nothing didn't understand human tongue. It had no need to.

If the man had been slightly more aware of his surroundings, he would have noticed the animals of the woods fleeing where the Nothing was. Instinct told them that *something* was about to happen, in the way that animals know about earthquakes just before the ground trembles.

A large buck bounded gracefully over a fallen log, two yearlings in close pursuit. A mischief of raccoons led a small parade, complete with a possum and three skunks. The owl, having caught its dinner in its beak, rested briefly on a limb to swallow it whole before taking flight again.

The animals knew something that the man did not.

Something was going to happen in these woods tonight, and they did not want to be in the vicinity when it did.

3

The whiskey was gone.

Walking through the woods turned out to be thirsty work, Eric discovered, and with no foresight to bring any water, Eric had no choice but to drink what he had on hand. When the last drop was drunk, Eric tossed the bottle aside. It smashed against a mossy boulder, the sound of breaking glass standing out starkly in his quiet surroundings.

He was too drunk to notice the weight of the silence that had settled into the woods, and he was making a great deal of noise, crashing clumsily through the brush. Gone were his careful footsteps, they took far too much concentration than he was currently capable of. It took most of his focus just to stay upright and on his feet.

Eric was sweating despite the chill of the evening. He wiped his brow on the sleeve of his sweatshirt. His breath burned in his lungs, reminding him of when he was a child, running around on the playground during recess in the wintertime. He tried to catch his breath and breathe through his nose, but that would require him either slowing his pace or stopping altogether.

If he had stopped, he would have noticed how quiet and still the woods had become.

Eric had been walking for an hour. If he had walked in a straight line, he would soon have found his way out of the woods and into his neighbor's apple orchard. Instead, he had walked in a wandering spiral, his path sometimes crossing over itself as he periodically looked up at the sky to see if he could still see the glow on the horizon.

He was deep in the woods now, on the far end of the spiral he had subconsciously been making. Eric turned his head skyward but was unable to see anything besides the dark, wooded ceiling of branches.

A needle of panic slid into his chest as Eric realized he was disoriented. He didn't know which direction he had come from or which part of the sky he was checking for the glow of the city lights.

Everything looked the same in the dark. Eric didn't want to admit it to himself, or even finish thinking the thought. He tried to distract himself from it, but the reality set in regardless of his denial.

Eric was lost.

His head began to swim as adrenaline entered his bloodstream. It helped knock out some of the cobwebs caused by the whiskey, but it also felt like he was being pulled in opposing directions from the inside out. The alcohol wanted him to sit and wait it out, but the adrenaline kept him on his feet and moving.

He broke into a run, fear overriding any logic he may have had remaining in his brain.

As he ran, he thought of Monica.

If he didn't find his way out of the woods, would she put a search party together to find him?

Eric sincerely doubted it.

The last time they spoke was earlier in the week before his phone service shut off. The conversation had ended with expletives from both sides. Eric had been late with his alimony payments for the past few months, but he always made good on them and professed that should be enough.

"The judge said every two weeks. Not once a month. Not whenever you feel like it. Every two weeks," Monica had said over the phone.

"I know what the judge said, but I would appreciate some flexibility right now," Eric replied. He wasn't a very prideful man, but it was embarrassing to admit to his ex-wife that he was struggling financially. "I've been late making the deposits recently because I'm in a bit of a rough patch."

There was a pause and a shift in Monica's tone. "I'm sorry. I had no idea. You should have said something earlier."

They had had their fair share of differences since the affair, but this surprised Eric. He didn't think she'd give him any slack whatsoever.

"I didn't want to tell you because I didn't want you

to think I was making excuses, but . . ." Eric trailed off.

He hadn't told her about losing the house. He hadn't told anyone, actually. Not his parents, not anyone at work. He wasn't sure she even deserved to know, but maybe she would give him some relief, at least for a little while.

"I'm losing the house," he said at last.

Monica gasped, and then there was silence on the line.

Eric heard Trent in the background.

"What is it, Mon?" he asked.

"You're losing the house?" Monica asked, ignoring Trent. "How long do you have?"

Eric was about to respond when he heard Trent laugh.

"What a fuckin' loser," he said, chuckling.

Eric closed his eyes, trying to remain calm, trying to ignore Trent's comment.

"I have about two weeks before they lock me out. It would be extremely helpful if you let me take a pass on this month's alimony. I need to find a place, and once I get back on my feet, I'll get caught up on—"

"Sure, of course, Eric. I wish you had said something sooner. We could have worked something out."

Trent spoke up from the background again.

"The fuck we couldn't!" Trent objected. His voice got louder, indicating he was moving closer to Monica.

Eric started to lose his grip on his patience. "Can you tell your boyfriend to butt out? This conversation doesn't involve him."

There was a rustle on the phone, and Monica's

voice muffled. "Trent, babe, just go in the other room. I'll be done in a second."

There came a fleshy smack and a brief cry of pain. Monica must have dropped the phone when Trent hit her because there was a loud clattering sound. Loud, angry, and indistinguishable words were exchanged, and then heavy, retreating footsteps.

Then Monica was back on the line. She sniffled, a sound Eric knew from a decade of marriage meant she was crying.

"You're going to let him treat you like that?" Eric asked.

"Eric, don't. I don't want to hear it. I'm fine."

He sighed, exasperated. "If you say so. This was all your choice anyway," he reminded her. She made her bed, and now she had to lie in it.

"You need to make your alimony payment on time or else I'll file a motion in court to garnish your wages," Monica said. Her voice was hollow, as if she was reciting someone else's words. Eric suspected they were Trent's.

"What happened to flexibility?" Eric asked, disheartened but not surprised by her reversal.

"Trent said no."

"And you always do what Trent says? Because he beats you if you don't?"

That struck a nerve.

"Please, Eric . . ."

"Don't think you can come crying to me if he gets too rough on you one night. He's the one you wanted to be with, remember?"

"Eric—"

"The Monica I knew wouldn't have tolerated that. I hope you wise up and leave that asshole before he beats you to death."

"Will you shut up?" Monica yelled. "You have some nerve, judging me when you're the one who's going to be homeless next week."

The two of them traded insults for the next few minutes until Eric realized that trying to negotiate with her was pointless. She was under Trent's thumb now.

"Forget I even offered to help you," Monica said as if she read his mind. "Fuck you, Eric."

She spit the words out, dripping with so much venom that Eric flinched on his end of the line.

"You are such a bitch, no wonder you like being on a leash. Good fucking riddance."

He ended the call.

And now, lost in the woods and replaying the conversation over in his mind, he determined that the likelihood of Monica wondering where he disappeared to was slim to none.

He had paid the alimony payment within moments of ending the phone call if only to avoid the threat of wage garnishment. He didn't think Monica would follow through with such a threat, but with Trent at the wheel, anything was possible.

Making the payment left him with only $23.00 in his bank account, which he diligently saved through the week until earlier in the evening. He used most of that remaining balance to buy a cheap bottle of whiskey on his way home from work. Earlier in the evening, Eric thought that drinking whiskey for dinner, sitting on the porch of the home he was losing to foreclosure, was a new low for him.

Now, nearing midnight, drunk and alone and lost in the woods, he was pretty sure this was it.

Eric slowed his run to a jog and then stopped completely. He leaned forward, putting his hands on his knees, and tried to catch his breath. Sweat dripped down his forehead, stinging his eyes.

He closed his eyes, rubbing the sweat off his face with his shoulder. When he opened his eyes again, he was looking straight down at the ground.

As his eyes readjusted to the gloom, he noticed a beetle scurrying along the ground. Its wiry legs scuttled rapidly at a speed that seemed to be unusual for an insect. Just behind the beetle was a myriad of other bugs: ants, spiders, grasshoppers, even a cicada. They were all moving, and they were all moving in the same direction.

Eric looked up, following the stream of insects with his eyes. He saw that it was more than just bugs on the move. He saw a variety of animals, big and small, all running together as if they were running away from something.

The fine hairs on Eric's arms and the back of his neck stood up.

His brain worked furiously to try to make sense of what he was seeing. He knew it wasn't normal but he couldn't identify the severity of what would cause all forms of life to flee the woods. The understanding of what was happening was impeded by a wall of fog. As he struggled to think, he felt something crawl over his right foot. He looked down and saw a small fox sprinting to catch up with the herd.

Then, there was a grunting sound behind him to his left. Startled, Eric turned to see what had made the sound.

A doe was standing about fifty feet away. Its large, distended belly indicated to Eric that it was pregnant. This was the closest Eric had ever been to a deer, and the first time he had seen a pregnant deer at all. He was embarrassed to realize he didn't know that deer even made noise. He was overcome by the rarity of what he was experiencing, but as that faded, he realized there must be a reason this deer wasn't joining the other animals around him fleeing like a great flood was coming.

The doe sidestepped a little, all but one of its feet changing positions. One of its hooves stayed firmly attached to the ground. Eric squinted to see, but in the dim lighting, it looked as if the deer had gotten its foot stuck between some rocks.

Without thinking, Eric approached the deer to see if he could help get it unstuck. The doe was clearly agitated, and the closer Eric got, the more the deer surged against its trapped foot. It grunted and whined, spittle flying from its mouth. Its motions became increasingly violent and severe, borderline epileptic. Eric grimaced when he saw a red stain forming around its trapped leg.

He paused, still about thirty feet away, hoping the deer would calm down. The doe did stop yanking on its leg, and Eric was relieved. The deer's leg had been making a horrible grating sound as it tried to work itself free. Eric was afraid its leg would break with a sickening snap like so many fallen and dried out tree limbs that he himself had stepped on during his nighttime nature hike. He didn't want to think about what the fate of a pregnant doe with a broken leg would look like.

The doe's respite was short-lived. Even though Eric hadn't moved at all except to breathe, the deer began to pant. Its tail flipped up and down, and it began to paw at the ground with its front hooves. Slowly at first, but then faster. It began grunting again, but it was a deeper, more guttural sound. Eric looked on as the doe began to shake its head violently from side to side.

Suddenly, the doe surged against its trapped leg. It threw its entire weight, and its leg snapped below the knee. Eric saw bone tear out of the brown hide, and the doe bleated in pain. It fell over onto its side, its front legs ceaselessly pawing at the air. The bottom part of its broken leg remained trapped in the rocks, and with the deer now on its side, the rest of its leg was rendered into a severe angle that made Eric's stomach somersault.

He wanted to turn away because watching the doe suffer was not something Eric thought he could handle. He momentarily forgot about being lost in the woods, forgot about his financial troubles. The only problem at hand was the pregnant deer with a compound fracture in its left hind leg. He wasn't sure what he was capable of doing to help the deer, but he couldn't just stand there.

Eric took one step toward the doe and it began seizing. Thrashing, twisting, convulsing on the ground with such rapid motions that the broken parts of its leg split completely in two, blood spurting out of the splintered stump.

Bile rose in Eric's throat as a peculiar smell filled the air. He recognized it almost instantly, and a wave of dread passed over him. It was the smell of burnt hair. A quick flash of a memory brought him back to his childhood when his older sister burned off her bangs with a curling iron. The smell had filled their home, had filled his nostrils like it was now. Except how? Eric didn't see any fire or feel any heat.

Fire or not, he could see the doe's fur smoldering in front of him. The clouds overhead parted, and in this small clearing, it allowed for the moonlight to provide a clear view of what was happening. Its fur was slowly turning black, the smolder spreading across it like watercolor paint. By the time its torso was completely enveloped, the doe had stopped thrashing.

Whatever it was, it was killing the deer. Given the state of its leg, it was a blessing in disguise. The doe was still breathing, but it had become shallow and labored, and it gradually slowed in frequency. Eric heard two slight popping sounds and noticed that the doe's eyes had ruptured.

With that, the doe lay still, a fine smoke rising off of its pregnant belly.

The smell of burnt fur and coppery blood was so strong, Eric could taste it. He was grateful the doe wasn't suffering anymore but was reeling from having beheld its gruesome death. It was unnatural, the blackness taking it over like a shadow, and he was glad it was over.

Except that it wasn't.

Eric had turned on his heel to go back the way he came when he heard another noise behind him. It sounded wet, and something was stretching and tearing. He didn't want to turn back but felt compelled to.

There was movement coming from within the dead

doe's belly.

With sickening realization, Eric understood that just because the mother was dead, that didn't mean the child had died, too.

Eric saw something pushing out from within the charred fur. The skin stretched, a rivulet of blood issuing from a hole that appeared. A small black hoof extended out from the hole.

The hole made by the sharp hoof stretched and ripped open further as if whatever was inside the doe's womb was growing at a rapid rate. The deceased body of its mother rocked, its eyeless head looking like it was nodding in agreement. There was an anguished squeal. Steaming blood and entrails burst forth as the doe's belly ruptured.

A small fawn tumbled out onto the forest floor in a gush of glistening organs, covered in placenta.

Revolted, Eric leaned forward and vomited at his feet. The voiding of the alcohol in his stomach, combined with the shock of watching a shocking death and simultaneous birth, had an intensely sobering effect on him. He wiped his mouth on this sleeve and felt his mind sharpen.

The fawn squirmed in a heap on the ground, a tangle of skinny legs and umbilical cord. It tried getting to its feet, but the fawn's muscles didn't seem strong enough to support its weight. It struggled to find balance, and after a few false starts, stood up on wobbly legs. It had cut itself on the rocks and was bleeding from a large wound on its flank.

The fawn leaned down and drank from the

spreading pool of blood, a mixture of its mothers and its own. Once it had its drink, it turned to face Eric and he saw a set of bony nubs protruding out of its skull.

The antlers were growing. Like he was watching it in time-lapse, a broad set of antlers grew up and out from the top of its head. Surely the weight of them would have been too much for the newborn fawn to bear, yet it remained standing in defiance of that logic.

Each point spread and spawned its own branch, and soon, there was a massive rack that more resembled a thick tumbleweed than antlers. Growing in symmetry, twin offshoots curled upward and back down toward the fawn's face, piercing its eyes. *Like mother, like son*, Eric thought perversely, and gagged as the antlers continued through, pushing its brains out the back of its soft skull.

The same blackening began to happen to the fawn. Even though by now it was surely dead, brains oozing down its neck, the fawn began screaming. It trembled as the antlers continued to split and spread, piercing its torso and exiting its chest.

Eric turned, slipping on the pile of his vomit. It felt oddly hot, juxtaposed with the chill of the night. As he gathered himself, he heard the fawn explode behind him. Unknown wet debris, hot and putrid, pelted him on his back and neck. The woods fell deathly quiet, and that was almost more unsettling than the death of the two deer.

The woods, at night or day, is never quiet.

His mind, he understood now why he had seen every living thing running in the same direction.

They were running away from the spreading darkness that was behind him in the woods.

Something that burned you alive, something that caused horrible mutations, something that caused you to rupture from the inside out.

Eric began walking, and after a few steps, he began jogging. The jogging soon became running, and then he was in an all-out sprint.

Away from the doe and her fawn who were quickly disintegrating, absorbing into the thirsty soil, and away from the spreading darkness that lapped at his heels.

4

Eric wasn't sure how long he had been running or how far he had gone. None of that really mattered to him as his only priority was to keep ahead of whatever was causing the blackened, burning moss to spread. Even with all of his troubles, despite his fleeting, flirtatious thoughts of suicide, the last thing he wanted was to suffer the same fate as that poor doe.

He sprinted for as long as he could. His lungs burned as he pushed himself beyond the limits he thought he was capable of. Whenever he thought he couldn't run any further, he would remind himself of what he had just seen.

The doe's pregnant belly bursting open.

The fawn's spiraling antlers pushing its brains through the back of its skull, reminding him horribly of his niece's Play-Doh toy.

That gave him the incentive to keep moving.

He ran until he came upon a large tree that had toppled over. The tree had taken several others down with it, creating an overlapping tangle of branches and trunk. He slowed to find a safe way to navigate around it.

He approached the fallen trees with caution. There were deep holes in the ground, left behind from the giant root balls being ripped up when the trees fell. They were easy to see, as the grouping of fallen trees created a window through the thick canopy, allowing for an unobstructed view of the night sky.

The moon was shining brightly through a copse of clouds. Compared to the darkness he had stepped out of, it felt like he was standing under a spotlight. Eric decided to take advantage of his current surroundings to rest. He climbed up onto one of the taller fallen trees, wanting a higher vantage point before he sat down.

Eric chuckled wryly despite the seriousness of his predicament, and for the first time, he considered how losing his home to foreclosure turned out to be a blessing in disguise. It was saving him the hassle of trying to sell a property that featured a vast expanse of demon-possessed woods.

After his lungs stopped burning and his heart stopped hammering in his chest, Eric remarked to himself again how unearthly quiet it was. The only sound was the wind and the creaking of the trees.

He scooted himself around in a slow circle, observing everything around him. He didn't feel safe where he was, but he needed to rest if he was going to make it out of the woods at all. He didn't think he'd feel safe even if he managed to get out of the woods and back into his home, knowing that something so terrible made its home in his backyard.

As he was completing his circle, he saw something protruding out of the ground, just to the edge of one of the voids caused by upturned roots.

It was a square granite pillar, standing proud from the earth nearly a foot. It was covered in scraggly moss. As he focused his eyes on it, he noticed something resting at the base of it. It looked like a backpack.

Eric jumped down from his perch and went over to it. Using a stick, he poked at the bag and turned it over. It was scorched and covered in mold, and it smelled of sulfur. Forgoing the stick, he nudged it with his toe.

The bag flipped over and knocked against something hollow. Eric saw it roll and land against the inside of his foot but couldn't see it behind his own shadow. He moved out of the way to allow the moonlight to show him what it was.

It was a skull.

A garbled yell strangled its way out of Eric's throat. He staggered back a few steps, almost falling backward into the shallow pit caused by one of the fallen pines. His arms wind-milled, trying in vain to restore his balance. His toes tottered on the edge of the pit. The dirt crumbled under his weight and he fell forward toward the skull.

He caught his fall on his elbows, wincing at the jarring impact he felt all the way up into his shoulders. He found himself eye-to-eye with the skull, noticing the burnt scraps of scalp and hair still clinging to it. In his periphery, he noticed a sprout of ribs half buried in the ground, as if the ground had gotten its fill partway through consuming the poor soul.

A moaning breeze swelled up behind Eric, reminding him of what he had been fleeing.

He scrambled to his feet, and without so much a thought, grabbed the backpack before leaving the group of fallen trees. He shrugged it onto his shoulder even though it smelled like death and rot. He didn't think he should leave it behind, as maybe there would be something useful inside.

Eric inadvertently kicked the skull as he moved away, and it rolled down underneath a root ball. A smoldering moss had crept in and was dripping off the roots, landing on the skull and spreading like thick ink.

Drop by drop, the skull burned.

5

Above the trees, above the clouds hiding the moonlight, the Nothing's eyes flared.

The longer it stayed in its current shape, the more damage it caused, both to itself and to its surroundings. None of that mattered, as fire was just as restorative as it was destructive.

It observed the man from above but also from below. It had eyes everywhere, even where eyes didn't exist. Until they burned closed, it could see through the dusty skull sockets of the surveyor.

The Nothing was discriminate about its prey.

It was bountiful within the man that was running

from the Nothing now, as well. It was in the smoldering shadows that slowly consumed the woods below.

It was what the Nothing was made of, at the coldest part of its core.

It sought what had spawned it into existence so very long ago.

The man in the woods on this night was rich with it, the volume of its presence almost deafening. It was what had woken the Nothing up from its hibernation because this particular flavor was not often felt, and it was magnetic.

A substance such as this was powerful. It was inebriating and all-consuming. It could be found in every part of the world, and it was in no short supply. The Nothing could sup anywhere it pleased, but everything else paled in comparison to what this man had. The surveyor, as enjoyable yet brief a repast he had been, was a mud puddle compared to this man's crystal ocean.

This man had it, and the Nothing needed, craved, *required* nothing more than every last bit of it.

6

The smell of the backpack faded after a while, though it wasn't just the smell that made Eric consider leaving it behind. The bag's material had a slimy, almost gelatinous texture to it. He had to make a conscious effort not to think about what had soaked into the fabric and into the cushioned straps, not to think about what made up the residue that seeped out onto his hands and clothes. He knew it was a lucky find and was grateful he had stumbled upon it.

When he realized he had blessedly gone nose-blind to its rugged odor, he decided to hang the bag on his chest so that he could rummage through it while he walked. He couldn't see much in the dark, but he made his way into a part of the woods where the trees weren't nearly as big, which allowed for more moonlight to make its way through. He felt around for the zipper to the main compartment and opened it.

Resting on top of the jumble of items was a water bottle. Eric grabbed for it, excited to find that it was half full. As much as his parched throat would have loved to down the entire contents, Eric exercised restraint and settled for a few sips. The water was lukewarm and reminded Eric of just how thirsty he was. He was tempted to drink more but put the bottle in a pouch on the side of the backpack.

He pressed on through the woods, walking slowly and checking his path often as he explored the rest of the bag. There was a binder full of laminated maps of Hamilton, but it only showed property lines. Eric recalled seeing a map similar to this hung on the wall at the Hamilton Town Office. Next to that was a Maine Gazetteer and several other road and topography maps. A cloth pouch was wedged next to all of the maps, and something metal and hard was inside. Eric felt a drawstring on the bag, pulled it open, and pulled out a collapsible metal shovel.

It was similar to one Eric had seen in a military surplus store when he was a teenager. The shovel blade folded where it met the handle shaft, which was connected to a wide, triangle-shaped handle. It had been clearly used quite a bit, as the business end was bent and scraped up. He put the shovel back into the backpack next to the maps. It would be useful if he needed to dig a latrine, but not much else he could think of.

Moving on to the small pocket on the front, Eric found a can of bug spray and a tube of sunscreen wrapped tightly inside of a Ziploc bag. There was a pocketknife with a serrated blade and a modest first aid kit inside a zippered pouch, and then his fingers brushed up against something with a knurled, metallic texture. Excited, he slipped the small flashlight out of its nylon sheath, clicking the button on the tail cap.

A narrow shaft of light sprung out, cutting through the darkness that had been surrounding him. The batteries were weak, he'd have to conserve them, but it was better than nothing. He switched the flashlight off and tucked it into the front pocket of his jeans.

The only other useful item inside of the backpack was a granola bar. Eric tore open the wrapper and ate it without giving a thought to the fact that it may have been expired or mold-ridden, or that it had been sitting in a backpack that had been stewing in liquid human remains for who knows how long. He barely tasted it, barely even chewed it before swallowing it down, grunting with pleasure. His empty stomach received the unexpected snack with a sharp growl. He rinsed it down with small sips of water and found himself feeling oddly content.

Eric wondered who the backpack belonged to. Based on the items in the backpack, he assumed the previous owner was a hiker of some sort, a survivalist or rural explorer that had somehow made it onto this property.

Eric hadn't gotten around to posting NO TRESPASSING signs, but he felt a sliver of irritation at the thought of an uninvited stranger on his land. A pang of guilt almost immediately replaced it, remembering that, invited or not, the person had met death on his land.

He silently thanked the stranger for their unintentional gift.

Eric realized he had stopped walking. Distracted by the items he found inside the backpack and lost in thought, his pace had slowed until he was standing still. Eric looked around, searching for the spreading, smoldering blackness he was fleeing from.

As he looked around, the moonlight rapidly faded into complete darkness like a curtain had been drawn. His feeling of being content evaporated in an instant, his heart jumpstarted by fear as he stood in a darkness so wholly void of light that it was dizzying. A chill raced through him as he reached for the flashlight in his pocket, and with trembling hands, he clicked it on.

The flashlight cut a swath into the dark, and Eric saw a rolling black fog. It consumed everything in its path, reducing brush and ferns to ash. It lit up the fieldstone buried under the topsoil, becoming streaks of magma that glowed red and orange yet somehow shed no light at all. It was the same black smolder that Eric had seen overcome the doe, and it was now coming for him.

It was closer to him now than it ever had been, but instead of running from it, Eric stayed where he was. It was entrancing, watching the spreading fog as it rolled up the small knoll he was standing on. It curled and boiled over itself, as if each billowing furl was competing with the next. It was almost at his ankles when Eric snapped out of his trance.

He jumped back several steps, keeping his eyes and his flashlight trained on the spreading smolder. As he spun the backpack so that it rested on his back instead of his chest, one of the straps tore free. The backpack dropped to the ground, its contents spilling out.

The smolder spread forward, eager to take from Eric the items that might have aided in his survival. The maps, the shovel, the bottle of water, whatever else may have been inside that he hadn't found yet, all of it blackened and burned.

Before it consumed the backpack entirely, Eric bent down and snatched the pocketknife from the front flap. He stuffed it into his pocket and stepped back. The backpack flashed a black flame as it was swallowed up.

Eric turned away from the spreading burn. He knew he had to start running again but wasn't sure he had any strength left in his body to manage more than a few steps.

He settled for that—one plodding step after another.

He supposed he didn't have to run all out, he just had to move faster than the smolder. His body and mind exhausted, Eric formulated a plan.

Facing away from the smolder, Eric aimed his flashlight into the woods ahead of him. He memorized as much of what laid ahead as he could and switched off the flashlight to conserve its battery.

The night surrounded him in an instant. He took several cautious steps forward, trying his best to remember the obstacles on the ground ahead. An exposed root to his left, a jagged stump on the right, a low hanging branch a few feet ahead.

Every fifty steps, he would allow himself a few seconds of light from the flashlight so that he could both make sure he was keeping far enough ahead of the smolder and to see what else lay ahead to map out his path.

It was slow going, but Eric hoped he only had to keep this up until daybreak.

Whenever that was.

7

Monica laid awake in bed.

Trent was snoring loudly beside her, dead to the world, oblivious to the fact that she was awake or that she had never fallen asleep to begin with.

It's not that she wasn't tired, but her headache made sleep impossible.

The headaches were becoming a familiar thing. They were the kind that could only be cured by sleep, assuming you could get any.

She licked her lips and winced. She had somehow forgotten about her broken and scabbed bottom lip, a gift she received earlier that night from Trent. It throbbed and was hot and swollen. He had delivered this gift swiftly from the backside of his hand when she had the audacity to tell him he had had enough to drink. He disagreed and didn't take kindly to being told what to do.

His beatings had become a familiar thing, too.

He began pushing her around not long after they

had moved in with each other. Monica thought he was just being playful, like how the boys teased their crushes on the schoolyard playground when she was a child, except maybe he didn't know his own strength. The pushing became shoving, and then the shoving became hitting, and before she knew it, Monica found herself making excuses for her injuries whenever someone at work asked her about them.

Not many people asked if she was okay anymore. Her circle of friends had thinned out significantly, as Monica had alienated nearly all of them. Trent didn't like her spending time with anyone else but him. He had a wild jealous streak and was extremely controlling, so to avoid any more conflict than she already had in her life, Monica let her friendships lapse.

The drinking and the beatings went hand in hand. The more he drank at night, the more brutal the beatings were. He only beat her when he got drunk, which didn't happen all that often at first. He used to only get drunk once a month or once every ten days, and that was something she told herself she could live with.

But of course, his drinking inevitably got worse, and so did the beatings.

The fact that she was willing to accept any abuse at all was the surest of signs that she needed help. She was caught in the confines of an abusive relationship, and like most people who find themselves in such a place, Monica couldn't see a way out.

She had wanted this, after all.

Well, not the abusive boyfriend part.

She had left a good and stable (but exceedingly

boring and loveless) relationship to be with Trent. She had always felt that her marriage to Eric was finite and she was just biding her time until the end came around. He was a good husband, kind and selfless and loyal, but he was never what she wanted.

When she met Trent, it was a scandalous thrill that reunited her with her youth. It lit a spark inside her she had never felt with Eric. At first, Trent felt like the kind of guy she should have married instead of playing it safe with Eric. That wistful regret pushed her closer to Trent and further from Eric, who was oblivious to her infidelity until the day he wasn't.

She had been living on both sides of the fence for far too long and had to pick a side.

How was she to know Trent wouldn't turn out to be the man he both seemed and promised to be? He had hid his latent alcoholism from her quite well until it was too late to change her mind.

Monica didn't regret leaving Eric, as she had inwardly thought of their marriage to be like a sick family dog. The end was coming one way or another, and she felt it was better to euthanize it than to prolong the pain.

What she did regret was leaving Eric for the asshole who lay asleep beside her, passed out drunk with knuckles bruised from hitting her.

She hated Trent.

She hated that she had become a cliché because of him, but she had made this bed and now she had to lay in it.

She chuckled silently at the irony of her situation.

Monica had become good at hiding the bruises on her arms, but it was next to impossible to cover a split lip.

Aside from the headache, Monica was kept awake on this night, fervently trying to come up with a cover story that she could tell anyone who asked her about it.

It occurred to her that icing her lip might help, so she slid carefully off the bed and grabbed her phone from her nightstand. She was careful not to make any sudden moves when getting off the bed, as the last thing she wanted was to wake Trent up. He needed to sleep off the twelve-pack and the half bottle of vodka he had polished off.

She tiptoed across their bedroom floor, picking out the spots on the floor that she knew didn't make a squeak or creak underfoot. She eased the bedroom door closed behind her and then made her way out to the kitchen.

Monica found an icepack in the freezer and wrapped it in a paper towel. She sat at the kitchen table, the one she and Eric had bought together that she kept when she moved out, and applied the icepack to her broken lip. She felt a tooth flex in her gums and winced. He had hit her harder than she had originally thought. No wonder her head hurt, she probably had a concussion.

It was probably a blessing in disguise that she couldn't sleep.

She sat at the table for more than an hour, scrolling through her Instagram feed. It was a mindless activity, good for taking her thoughts off her injury and her abusive boyfriend. The icepack eventually melted, and when Monica got up to put it back in the freezer, she saw a bottle of vodka resting next to a bag of frozen mixed vegetables.

She considered it for a moment and then decided to help herself to a nip. Mixing alcohol with a mild concussion probably wasn't a good idea, but she only wanted enough to help her fall asleep. She stood at the freezer with the door open and slipped her phone into the pocket of her cotton shorts. She grabbed the bottle and unscrewed the cap.

"What do you think you're doing?"

Monica stopped, the vodka bottle just before her swollen lip. Her heart leapt into her throat.

"Trent, I'm—"

"You're what? Thirsty?"

She turned to face him. Trent stood in the doorway to the kitchen, eyes swimming in red. He had to hold onto the side of the doorframe to steady his balance, but still, he swayed on his feet.

"No, I only wanted a sip. I've got an awful headache and thought it might help."

Trent walked on unsteady feet across the kitchen and snatched the vodka out of her hands. The bottom of the bottle clipped Monica's wrist, connecting with bone and resonating up her arm. She bit her lip to keep from moaning in pain, piercing through the scab, and she tasted fresh blood. She took a few steps backward and bumped up against the counter.

"This is *mine*," Trent said.

"I know, babe. I'm sorry. I wasn't thinking," Monica replied, trying to keep her voice steady, her tone submissive.

"That's your problem, Mon. You don't think."

Trent put the bottle to his lips and took a large gulp. When he was done, he threw the bottle to the floor. It shattered, showering them both with vodka and broken glass. Monica screamed briefly before clapping her hands over her mouth.

Trent's eyes snapped open with rage. He hated it when she made loud noises when he beat her. He didn't want nosy neighbors invading his privacy. A dog in the apartment next door started barking, and a scowl grew across his face.

An ocean of broken glass separated Trent from Monica, another blessing in disguise. They both were barefoot and they stared at each other in silence as they waited to see if anyone would come knocking at their door.

Monica hoped desperately that someone would, as she did every time Trent beat her. She prayed to hear footsteps approach the door, to hear someone knock to see if everything was okay, but no one ever did.

There was a look in Trent's eyes that scared Monica. He looked at her with glassy hatred, an expression that Monica knew from experience meant he was getting ready to throw his fists around. Except something was different tonight. He seemed . . . disconnected.

He bent down and picked up the broken neck of the vodka bottle from the floor. With a lopsided and grim smile, he walked across the kitchen toward her. Broken glass pierced the bottoms of his feet, leaving behind smears of blood.

During the last two years of living with Trent, Monica had endured many beatings. She had been thrown into walls and against corners of tables. She had suffered countless bruises and scrapes, a broken finger, and a dislocated shoulder. Earlier tonight, she received a split lip and a concussion from him, and she was pretty sure from the rapid bruising and swelling that the vodka bottle had broken something in her wrist.

His beatings were something she used to accept as a part of her life, but seeing him approach her now, wielding a shard of glass like a diminutive sword, a dormant survival instinct kicked in.

It was a stroke of luck that Monica stood on the side of the kitchen closest to their front door. She grabbed for her purse that hung near the door and made a run for it.

Trent roared from behind her. He crossed their small kitchen in a few strides, grabbing the back of Monica's t-shirt as she unlocked the door and threw it open.

"You're not going anywhere," he grunted through gritted teeth.

Monica fell back toward him, caught at the throat by the collar of her t-shirt. She gripped her hands tightly on the doorframe, refusing to be pulled back in. Her injured wrist exploded with pain, but she gritted her teeth and did not allow herself to let go.

Trent slashed at her back with the broken bottle. The sharp edge cut easily through her shirt, which ripped off of her as she lunged forward and fell out into the hallway. A hot line of fire traced across her back and she felt a trickle of blood follow the indent of her spine down to her waist. Tears sprung to Monica's eyes, but she blinked them away.

In the hallway outside Trent's apartment, Monica spun around. Trent stood in their kitchen, holding her ripped t-shirt in one hand and the broken bottleneck in the other, the tip red with blood. Her blood.

"If you leave, you're as good as dead to me," Trent said, his voice low and wavering but distinct.

"Not much would be different if I stayed," Monica replied.

She was grateful for the foresight she had to put on a workout top underneath her t-shirt before going to bed. The formfitting tank top was now cut open in the back, but at least she wasn't rendered topless by losing her t-shirt.

Purse in hand, Monica left Trent standing in the doorway. She didn't care that she was barefoot. She didn't care that she was about to go out into the cold night air, wearing only cotton shorts and a tank top. She didn't care that her lip was busted, that her wrist was broken, or that she was bleeding from a slash cut into her back that would likely require stitches.

She had made it out. She wasn't going to wind up as one of those statistics she saw on the posters about domestic abuse in the breakroom at work that made it look so easy. As if leaving an abusive situation was as simple as making a phone call for help.

No, you had to be ready to leave everything behind, and hopefully before your abuser took what mattered most: Your life.

Monica was fortunate to have more than that. She had her car keys and her cell phone.

"You're as good as dead!" Trent reminded her loudly this time. Loud enough for the neighbors to hear.

Monica laughed for just a second, forcing herself to stop when she felt the cut on her back tear open further as her lungs expanded.

She stepped out into the cold night air and began

shivering almost immediately. Monica wasn't sure if it was just from the temperature or from shock. Regardless, she walked quickly to her car, trying to avoid stepping on anything painful along the way.

Before getting behind the wheel, Monica looked over her shoulder to see if Trent had followed her. The parking lot, save for the vehicles belonging to the other tenants and Trent's oversized pickup, was empty. She went to her trunk and rummaged around, knowing she had two items buried in the clutter that would help her immensely.

"Aha!" she said out loud when she found them: a pair of sandals and a zip-up sweatshirt.

She dropped the sandals onto the ground and slid her feet in. The sweatshirt was next, but she wasn't sure she could navigate her damaged wrist through the sleeve. Instead of putting her arms through, she opted to just drape it over her shoulders.

Behind the driver's seat now, she started the engine, realizing then that she didn't have one important thing:

A place to go.

Monica put the car in reverse and backed out of her spot. A destination was irrelevant at this point. She really only needed to get away from Trent. She would figure the rest out once she was on the road.

The cut on her back was on fire. She could feel the blood soaking into the sweatshirt, hardening and clotting the fabric. Monica briefly considered going to the hospital, but the thought of going through all that alone terrified her.

There would be questions, and lots of them. She didn't have the mental stamina to withstand such a presumably rigorous process alone. She knew she would have to go eventually, but not right now.

It was almost midnight. Tears formed in her eyes when she realized that through Trent, she had pushed everyone that was good for her away. She was alone in this.

Monica drove around Hamilton. The city was quiet, asleep. She drove past a dive bar named *Paulie's* and saw a middle-aged man locking the door. He raised a hand and waved, smiling at her as she drove by his empty parking lot. She attempted a smile but wasn't sure how convincing it was.

Her mind wandered, and she thought about Eric and the last conversation she had with him. It wasn't exactly the most pleasant memory to bring up, but the night had been full of pain from the beginning.

You are such a bitch, no wonder you like being on a leash.

He had asked her for help and Monica denied it, bowing to Trent's demand. Knowing Eric as well as she thought she did, he must have been in a bad way to actually ask for help. He wasn't a prideful man, but he had to be really suffering to even think about reaching out.

Monica knew she had burned all of her bridges with Eric, but she put her blinker on and pointed her car in the direction of his house anyway. The situation she found herself in was an extreme one, but despite the bad blood between them, she didn't think he would turn her away. Lord knows she had certainly given him enough reasons to.

Not ever the religious type, she said a prayer as she drove that Eric would take her in.

Already in a great deal of pain as it was, she figured it couldn't hurt.

8

Trent was in a furious cloud of disbelief that Monica actually left.

After all he had done for her, was *still* doing for her, it was an outrageous concept to him that she would be so thankless and selfish.

"Fucking Monica," he said to his empty kitchen.

He gripped the broken vodka bottleneck so tightly that it cracked in his hand. He dropped it to the floor and watched it skitter around and roll under the stove.

His head was a swamp of half-finished, incoherent thoughts, each of them bubbling with anger. He had a headache so strong that it felt like he had an ax buried between his eyes, and it made his vision dance around a little when he tried to look at something.

His feet hurt, too.

He had stepped on the broken glass as a show of how strong he was, how unstoppable he was. It was meant to be intimidating, a foolish idea he wasn't sure had its desired effect. Monica still left, after all. It may have been a badass thing to do, but now, the bottoms of his feet were all cut up. He hobbled backward and fell into a chair at the kitchen table. He used his dirty fingernails to dig out a few shards that had sunk into the thick, calloused skin.

The room spun around him as he tried to focus on his task. He didn't remember drinking enough to get this drunk. *Maybe that bitch dosed me with something,* he thought. *Or maybe I did drink that much.* Regardless of how he got there, he was close to blacking out.

A whisper of a memory surfaced and reminded him

that he hadn't always been a drinker. It was true, he never had a gluttonous taste for alcohol. Some beers with the boys, a shot or two to celebrate every now and then, nothing too crazy.

It wasn't like him to get blackout drunk on a Thursday night. That wasn't who he was.

It may not have been who he was, but that's who he was now.

He had always been a narcissistic asshole, but never an alcoholic narcissistic asshole.

Trent had stepped up from a social drinker to a full-blown alcoholic, and he knew exactly why he found himself with a habit he never thought he'd have:

He drank because when he was sober, he couldn't stop thinking about what he had dreamed about seeing in the woods behind Monica's ex-husband's house. The alcohol, when he'd had enough of it, made that all go away.

Trent had only been to Monica's ex-husband's house once: to help Monica pick up some boxes and things when she moved out. They had been screwing on the down-low for about a year at that point, and when their affair became public, he offered to let her move in with him. That was where he saw their relationship going anyway, even if it did feel a little premature at the time.

He had to put on a show, of course. That's just the kind of guy he was, not one to be outdone when it came to physical displays of masculinity. He never considered his bravado showmanship or the big truck as a means of overcompensation, but the handful of lovers he had before Monica who were left wholly dissatisfied might have said otherwise. He was just trying to assert himself.

When Trent had loaded up the last of the boxes into his truck, he went to exchange a few parting words with Eric. Monica cut him off at the pass.

"Just go wait in the truck, okay?" she asked.

He was going to protest, but he saw something behind her.

Trent could see into the backyard that led out to the massive spread of woods. There was a flash of motion that caught his eye. It was like a storm cloud, black and roiling through the trees. He saw something in the cloud that he didn't understand, beyond the fact that it absolutely terrified him.

That night, he dreamed of a man in the woods, splayed open from groin to chin, his lungs and heart sliding out of the cavern of his chest as the ground swallowed him up. He didn't know where the man's legs were. They were just gone. There was a steam rising from the corpse, and Trent thought it might have been the man's soul.

When he woke from the dream, he hoped that the memory of it would fade like the man's soul. Unfortunately, it stuck with him, flashes of it replaying when he closed his eyes. He was reminded of the man's face, mouth open in eternal pain, and the steam. The soul-steam.

That was part of the reason why Trent's drinking got out of control: to rid his consciousness (albeit temporarily) of what he had seen, and to forget that whatever caused that man's soul to evaporate was still out there in those woods.

Trent finished pulling glass out of his feet and put on a pair of sneakers. Leaning against the wall to help keep him upright, he went to the medicine cabinet in the bathroom and dry swallowed a handful of ibuprofen. His feet throbbed, and he could feel them swelling inside his shoes.

He made his way into his bedroom and sat down hard on the bed. Trent reached for his phone, rubbing his eyes to get them to focus on the screen.

Trent opened his app drawer and tapped on an app called *Trackit*.

An animated circle spun while the app loaded. After a few moments, a detailed map of Hamilton filled the screen and a green dot moved slowly across it.

Trent watched the green dot as it navigated around the map with seemingly no destination in mind. He sat and patiently watched it double back over itself more than once, and then it slowed to a stop.

The green dot was Monica's phone. He had installed a tracking app on her phone without her knowing months ago so he could keep track of where she was at all times. That was step two of the narcissist's handbook.

Being able to track her phone was the only reason why he let her leave and gave her such a big head start. He didn't chase her out or follow her in his truck because all he had to do was wait. Wait for the green dot to stop moving. He wasn't sure where she'd go, but he didn't think she was stupid enough to go to the hospital, despite whatever injuries he vaguely remembered inflicting upon her.

When the dot started moving again, it headed west.

"Don't you fucking dare," Trent said under his breath.

He had an idea of where she might be headed, and it was the one place he absolutely would not stand for.

Trent fished his truck keys out of his pocket.

It didn't matter that he was drunk and could barely stand. Trent just couldn't let that happen. That bastard had divorced *her*, and Monica was Trent's now.

"You're as good as dead, Mon."

9

Eric, who had started his walk in the woods to get away from some of his problems, found several more along the way. To help keep himself awake and focused as he worked to stay ahead of whatever was chasing him through the woods, he ran down the list.

Divorced due to a cheating wife? Check.

Losing home to foreclosure? Check.

Lost in the woods with a possibly sprained ankle, being chased by a slow-moving burning fog that would surely kill him if he slowed down or stopped for even a second?

Check.

As if that wasn't enough, the way that his stomach was churning, Eric worried that he'd soon have another problem to add to the list.

The granola bar he had found in the dead man's backpack had turned. He wasn't sure if it was going to come back up or tear out of him in the other direction, but one thing he knew for sure: it wasn't a matter of if, but a matter of when.

Eric swallowed a mouthful of spit, his mouth seething from his upset stomach, and finished his fifty-count. He hit the switch on the end of the flashlight so he could map out his next fifty steps.

The flashlight didn't turn on.

He shook the flashlight and tried again, but still nothing.

Eric sighed and tossed the flashlight off to the side. It was useless to him now. The batteries had been on borrowed time, and much like the situation with his stomach, it was when, not if.

He was completely in the dark. Whatever moonlight there may have been earlier in the evening, there was absolutely none of it now.

Every time he had clicked on the flashlight, it was like the darkness was actively fighting against it. At the edges of its narrow beam, the darkness seeped in like it wasn't strong enough to hold its own. Eric was beginning to feel the same, worn out and pushed past his limit, except now, he couldn't see the darkness seeping in anymore because the darkness was everywhere.

Eric considered his options.

He was exhausted and scared. An hour ago, he thought he was more scared than anything else, but now, he wasn't so sure. Eric didn't think he had ever felt more tired than he did right now.

He stopped walking.

He didn't know how long it would be until the sun came up, but something told him it would be a while still. He didn't think he could walk for another couple minutes, much less another couple hours.

The last he checked, Eric was ten yards ahead of it, the spreading smolder. He wasn't sure how much time he had until it would be upon him, but he took the time he had left to think. Eric closed his eyes in acceptance of his fate, though it didn't make any difference at all.

He breathed in deep, filling his lungs, and turned to face what he had spent the entire evening in the woods running from. He tried thinking of what he had to live for but came up empty handed. He was divorced with no girlfriend, he had no children, and soon, he would be homeless.

Now that he was still, Eric could hear the smolder as it crept along the ground toward him. Crackling, rustling, hissing. He braced himself, steeling his nerves for when it would slide over his feet, crawl up his jeans. It would fuse his clothing to his skin, melting the fabric into his flesh before his flesh melted off of his bones. He wondered if it would hurt, forgetting how much pain the doe appeared to have been in before it had been overcome.

The noise of his approaching death grew louder and Eric felt a shift in the temperature of the air around him. It was warm, and getting warmer fast. Claustrophobia set in, and that was all Eric needed to realize that, tired or not, pity party be damned, this wasn't how he wanted to go.

Eric opened his eyes, and that's when he saw it:

A clearing in the woods.

It was off to his left, and the moonlight was shining so brightly that Eric thought at first a searchlight was shining down from the sky, hanging off a rescue helicopter that had been dispatched to find him. The light wasn't from a helicopter; it was from the moon.

The clouds had been stripped away, and the opening that Eric saw through the trees was a stage. The moon, a spotlight. Compared to the pure darkness he had been plotting his path through, the moonlight made his eyes water.

A searing heat cut through his sneaker as the smolder took its first bite.

Eric yelled in pain and surprise.

He yanked his foot back. He stumbled backward, almost losing his balance and falling over. That would have been the end, for sure. Instead, he threw his weight toward the clearing and fell into a stumbling run.

The pain in his foot was intense. He could feel his toes blistering and swelling inside his shoe, and each step shot needles of pain up his legs. Adrenaline surged through him so strongly, he could taste it. A bitterness that both pushed him forward and dulled the roaring pain in his foot.

Eric crashed his way through the brush. The closer to the clearing he got, the more important to him the clearing became.

The Clearing was safety. The Clearing was where he could finally rest.

The Clearing was where the smoldering fog couldn't get him.

That last thought surprised and confused Eric. He didn't know where it came from. Desperate hopefulness, perhaps, but a lot of strange things had happened in these woods tonight.

Eric hoped beyond hope that it was true.

Each step brought pain, but it also brought him

closer to the Clearing. That was a fair enough trade, so he kept going.

10

Shadows descended on the woods.

The Nothing had spread, reaching out and connecting with every part of itself it could. It no longer had any living creatures nearby to look through, as they had all fled the Nothing's shadow. Left with no other recourse, the Nothing had to rely on sensation alone to keep track of the man.

Locating him by feel was an easy task. The denser the tree growth, the more precisely it knew where the man was. Each root was a nerve ending, and each futile step the man made to get away sent a flurry of synapses along the intermingled web of roots to tell the Nothing exactly where he was. The man moved faster than the shadows did, but it didn't worry that he would escape.

No living thing ever escaped once the shadows set in, and definitely not once the Nothing had gotten a taste.

It managed to take two of the man's toes, and they were *divine*.

That was why the Nothing descended from its position so far above the woods. It wanted to get closer to the man, *needed* to get closer to him. It wanted to be on the ground so that when it finally had him, there was no undue delay in its consumption of him.

If the Nothing had a mouth, it would be drooling in anticipation.

11

Monica arrived at Eric's house and was surprised to find it completely dark. This seemed odd to her, as she remembered how he always left certain lights on in every apartment they ever rented together. Even if they were being conservative of their energy usage, he always insisted that at least the light above the kitchen sink be left on.

There were no exterior lights on, either. Her ex-husband's house practically disappeared in the night, swallowed up by the darkness that somehow seemed so much darker now that she was so far removed from the main parts of Hamilton. She almost drove by the house, so lost in the night it was.

She had tried calling Eric on her way over, but he hadn't answered. His voicemail didn't even pick up. Instead, she was greeted with a robotic message.

The wireless number you are trying to reach has been disconnected.

Monica hoped Eric wouldn't be too mad at her showing up unannounced and unwelcomed. She actually didn't care how mad at her he was, so long as he let her inside. She didn't mind eating a little crow if it meant she got a place to stay until she got her situation sorted.

Her headlights laid twin cones of light across the

house, reflecting the empty windows. She pulled into the driveway and parked in front of the garage. She put the transmission into park and shut her car off, forgetting about her wrist that was likely sprained, and grunted in pain.

Monica carefully climbed out of the driver's seat, cradling her throbbing wrist. She was pretty sure that the cut on her back had stopped bleeding, as her sweatshirt was stuck tight to her back with its scab. It pulled and tugged as she moved, reminding her that it was there in case the pain wasn't reminder enough. She clicked the flashlight app on her phone and made her way to the front door.

She hit the doorbell, but there was no sound from inside. She pressed it a few more times before giving up and knocked instead.

"Hello?" she asked, yelling into the door. "Eric, are you home?"

She didn't see his car in the driveway, but Eric was nothing if not predictable. She knew without needing proof that his car was parked in the garage. He wouldn't be out this late on a weeknight. Not with work the next day.

Monica counted to thirty before knocking again, harder this time. When there was still no response, she tried the doorknob. It was unlocked. Praying he hadn't armed the security system, Monica pushed open the door and let herself in.

"Eric, it's me," she called out into the dark house. "It's Monica."

Once inside, she threw the deadbolt and secured the chain lock across the door. Eric had often forgotten to lock the door before going to bed. He was always a heavy sleeper, too, which would explain why he hadn't heard her knocking. She sighed, a wistful smile crossing her face, speculating how some things just never change.

Her smile faded when she tried one of the light switches and nothing happened.

"Looks like your power is out," she said. "Must be a downed line somewhere."

Her voice echoed oddly in the dark house, but her senses were heightened and she tried not to think much of it. Monica used the light from her phone to navigate toward the master bedroom, silently rehearsing what she was going to say to Eric as she passed the living room. She cast a glance into it and stopped short.

It surprised her to see that the living room was empty, except for a crumpled sleeping bag and a pillow. There was no other furniture, not even drapes on the windows. The same went for every room, in fact. Empty of furniture, of any belongings of any kind.

"Eric? Are you home?"

The master bedroom was empty as well. Eric was nowhere to be found.

She backpedaled toward the garage, looking through the door that passed from the kitchen into the bays, and saw his car sitting there just like she suspected it would be.

Her heart churned in her chest, in part from fear and in part from concern for Eric. She spun in a small circle and saw the door that opened out to the back deck had been left wide open. Leaves cluttered the doorway, blown in from the wind. Without a second thought, Monica went to the door and stepped outside.

A dilapidated camp chair with an empty potato chip

bag stuffed into the cup holder was the only furniture she had seen thus far. It was Eric's favorite brand and, like the camp chair, was the only sign of him she had seen.

"Eric?" she called out. Her voice fell flat, carried off on the wind. "Eric!"

The wind offered no reply.

Monica trembled. The clouds parted. The moon shone down, casting a ghoulish light. She shielded her eyes with her good hand, looking out into the overgrown backyard. She scanned the tall grass that looked more like a hayfield than the putting green it had been the last time she saw it.

There, left of center, was a swath of grass that had been pushed down like someone had walked through it.

It had to have been Eric. Who else would have walked through his backyard?

The house sat on a plot of land that spanned more than a hundred and forty acres and there wasn't another soul around for miles.

Monica stood on the porch, considering her options.

She could go after Eric and try to find him in the woods. Wherever he was, he wasn't close enough to hear her yelling for him, and going out into the unknown with an injured wrist and slip-on sandals didn't sound like a wise idea.

Or, she could stay inside. Find a nice corner to fold herself into and wait for Eric to come back. The sun would be up in a couple hours and she was tired and in a great deal of pain.

She wrestled with what she wanted to do and what she felt she should do, or more accurately, what Eric would have probably done for her. That, combined with a feeling in her gut that she should keep moving, made up her mind.

Monica stepped down off the porch and followed Eric's path through the tall grass and into the woods.

12

Trent drove with the windows down.

The rush of the cold air aided him in two ways: It helped keep him awake and it sharpened his mind amidst the massive headache that was brewing.

He glanced at his phone, which was clamped in a docking station on his dashboard. The green dot that represented Monica's location had once again stopped and the *Trackit* app was narrowing in on it, telling him to turn left in half a mile. He didn't need to follow its directions to know where he was going.

The general vicinity of the green dot told him everything he needed to know.

Monica was in West Hamilton, on Running Valley Road. She had gone running back to her ex-husband just as he suspected she would. She was probably in bed with him right now, doing things with him under the covers. Maybe even things that she refused to do with him.

That train of thought only served to renew his anger. He goosed the gas pedal with his foot, the engine of his truck roaring in quick response. The RPM needle went up as he sped down the road, redlining before shifting into a higher gear.

Trent secured the steering wheel with his knee like he saw his father do countless times when he was a child. His father always hid a liquor bottle under the passenger seat, wrapped safely inside a brown paper bag. It wasn't until Trent was older that he understood what was in the bottle. When he was a kid, all he knew was that his old man's drink smelled bad. When dad drove with his knees, Trent knew he was going to take a pull from his bottle, and that was always when Trent buckled up.

He had learned how to drive with his knees from his father, and it turns out, his alcoholism was something he learned from him, as well.

Trent steadied the steering wheel and reached behind the passenger seat. He felt around for what he had hidden underneath the seat. When his fingers finally happened upon it, his mouth twisted into a slow smile.

Unlike his father, Trent's hidden item wasn't a liquor bottle.

It was something much more deadly.

13

At last, Eric made it to the Clearing.

He was nearly euphoric, but that might have been caused by light-headedness. He was breathing hard, but having convinced himself that all he needed to do was make it there and everything would be fine, he pushed himself past his furthest capacity. His lungs burned, his heart pounded, and the pain in his foot was unbelievable.

That was another distraction from reality, but one he could have done without. His entire right leg was a mass of cramped muscles and it would shake uncontrollably every time he put weight down on his foot.

Part of him knew it was an irrational thought, that the Clearing was a sanctuary that would save him from the shadows, but it gave him hope and he held on to that hope with whatever strength he could spare. Deep down, it was a coping mechanism to help him avoid accepting the reality that this ordeal was not going to be over soon, nor easily.

One thing he knew, especially based on his recent life experiences, was that if you are told the same lie often enough, eventually you start to believe it.

Monica was a liar, and she was fucking *good* at it. He hadn't seen it, not even in the slightest. Her affair with that asshole, Trent, completely blindsided him. But it wasn't just her infidelity she had been dishonest about.

It was her response to the thousands of questions he had asked. The things she said in the conversations they had. It was in her smile, her embrace, her love-making. It was in her eyes, her body language every time her phone went off. It was in her excitement over the house they were buying, the realization of a decade-long dream he thought they both shared.

There were a million little lies that all stacked up together to make the one Big Lie. A million cracks in the foundation of trust he had in the one person he should have been able to put full trust in. There were a million moments that were suddenly suspect, and the worst part about it was that even now, nearly two years after Monica's honesty bomb dropped and blew his life apart, those moments kept surfacing.

Every memory was a knife that cut him. Eric felt like he was covered in those cuts, and some of them would never heal. Some of them cut deeper than others.

Eric stopped walking when he reached the line of trees that separated the woods from the Clearing. When he first saw it through the trees, all he could think about was making his way to it. Now that he finally made it, he leaned against a tall pine to catch his breath.

The Clearing was more than just a clearing. It was a field in the middle of a forest, and in the middle of the field stood a cluster of narrow trees.

Eric thought back to when he had first found his house for sale on a real estate website. He looked up the address on Google Maps to find an aerial view. Aside from the acre or two the house sat on, the rest of the property was covered in trees. This large expanse of open field had not been there, hadn't been anywhere on the map to the best of Eric's recollection.

He was too tired to think about what may have caused the Clearing to appear. The entire way here, all he could think about was how inside, he could rest. Inside, it wasn't dark because the moon was shining.

Inside was asylum.

Eric stepped over the threshold into the Clearing, and in doing so, stepped out of the world as he knew it and

14

into somewhere else.

Inside the Clearing, Eric felt nothing.

There was no air on his skin. There was no sound, not even the ambient noise that exists even in traditional silence. It was ethereal and dreamlike and dangerously upending. The lack of input for his core senses created a slow building chaos that made it impossible for him to define what this place was.

It didn't feel like the nirvana he thought it was going to be.

He felt like an insect, stuck in a fathom of liquid amber that would soon harden around him and he would become a fossil, fully preserved for the wonderment of the archeologists that would discover him buried in a field sometime in the next millennium.

Eric turned around back toward the woods, deciding that he wanted to leave the Clearing. He wished he had never stepped into it, had never seen it in the first place, that he had let himself be consumed by the smolder.

Except the woods were gone. No, they were a speck of black in the distance, still there but impossibly far away. Somehow, without moving at all, he found himself standing in the middle of the field, that cluster of narrow trees just behind him. A rock covered in lichen was nearby and Eric sat down.

He tried to quell the panic and shock he could feel were trying to take over. This would-be asylum felt more and more like a trap with each passing second, but Eric knew he wouldn't have a chance of getting out if he lost his head. He closed his eyes and forced himself to concentrate. When he had formed a loose plan, he reopened them.

Self-assessment. That's what he would do first.

One thing Eric could still feel in this place was pain. The muscles all over his body ached, of course, but there was a problem with his foot. The one that had been touched by the smolder.

Eric hadn't been able to look at the damage until now, as it had been too dark. He carefully crossed his right leg over his left knee to take a look.

He was shocked to find that an entire corner of his shoe was gone. Not just his shoe, but the part of the foot that had been within it, too. Eric thought he had been off balance because of the pain, but the smolder had taken two toes at least. It was difficult to tell for sure. Everything was covered in thick, black dust, almost like soot but much stickier. The black powder spread up his foot and traveled up his leg to his thigh, wrapping around in tendrils like vines. Eric tried brushing it off but all he succeeded in doing was getting the black dust all over his hands.

His foot wasn't bleeding, which was good. From the looks of it, the smolder had auto-cauterized his foot as it took that part of him. Eric tried not to think of it as a bite, but that is what his mind kept going to.

Eric carefully put his injured foot on the ground and did an inventory of the rest of his body. A few scrapes and cuts from running through the brush, a sore ankle from tripping on that gopher hole, and a stomachache that wobbled on indecision. That rounded out the worst of it, assuming he didn't count how utterly exhausted he was.

Standing was a struggle, his fatigued muscles

crying out for rest. Eric knew that if he didn't stand up now, he wouldn't get back up. He stretched and breathed deep, unsure if it was air he was pulling into his lungs.

A low sound came from the cluster of trees behind him.

It was the first sound he had heard since he came into the Clearing. It was a grating hum, like the banks of transformers at an electricity substation. It swelled and slowed, sound waves lapping the shoreline. The sound vibrated through Eric, making his eyes lose focus and his teeth ache. It made every hair stand up, and it made his bowels turn to water inside him.

The sound intensified, and now Eric saw the cluster of trees begin to tremble. Their leaves fell to the ground, straight down as if in a vacuum instead of wafting and seesawing lazily down. It occurred to Eric then that what he thought he had been hearing, he was actually feeling instead. A concussive rush of energy exploded out from the trees. It hit Eric like a wall, knocking him flat on his back.

Eric rolled to his side and got to his knees in time to see a shadow descend from the sky. The shadow had a humanoid shape: a tapered torso with long arms, its head shrouded like it was wearing a heavy cloak.

It had eyes, two coals burning from underneath its hood.

15

Monica followed the path Eric had made through the tall grass. She wasn't sure how she was going to track him once she got to the woods, but if she was being honest with herself, she wasn't sure she was going into the woods to try to find him. She was in no shape to be traipsing around the woods, much less in the middle of the night.

She had hoped she would find Eric passed out somewhere in the backyard. Maybe he had gotten drunk and thought a stroll was a good idea but didn't make it as far as the woods. No such luck as she followed the grass he had matted down as he zig-zagged his way across. He was nowhere to be found.

That meant he had gone into the woods, after all.

Monica wrestled with going in after him or returning to the house. Maybe he was inside, and she had just missed him. She looked back at Eric's house. She could barely see it with all of its lights out, and then turned back to the woods.

Something in her gut told her that she needed to go in. The thought of wandering through the woods terrified her because it was so dark—

Monica spotted something bright between the trees.

It was a clearing and the moon was shining brightly upon it.

"Eric, are you out there?" she called.

There was no reply. The clearing didn't seem that far away, maybe a hundred yards at most.

The feeling she had in her gut told her that this bright clearing was where she needed to go. Maybe that's where Eric was.

Without any more hesitation, Monica decided to find out and stepped into the woods.

16

The Nothing watched as the man fell into its trap.

It had learned over the course of its time that humans were inquisitive. They had an innate desire to understand their surroundings, so if they saw something out of place, they would want to investigate.

If they saw a bright place when they had spent so much time surrounded by darkness, they would be drawn to it like moths to a flame.

Everything the man had done was predictable. From the moment it had caught the man's scent, the Nothing knew how this would end.

It would end as it always did. The Nothing was confident in that.

17

The stink of sulfur and wet dirt followed right behind the wall of energy that knocked Eric over. He gagged as he tried to stand up, instinctively pushing up off the ground with his bad foot. He groaned in pain.

The shadow figure with the burning eyes approached, and Eric struggled to comprehend what he was seeing. He wanted to believe that the shape that filled the sky, the one stalking him like a predator, was just a product of his exhaustion. No matter how many times he blinked or rubbed his eyes, the shadow remained.

Movement in the trees caught his attention. They shook violently as the shadow loomed.

Eric swung his eyes over to see the bark peeling off one of the trees in long strips, as if by unseen hands. It made a horrible ripping sound, the fibers of the bark stretching and tearing like scabs before letting loose. The tree bled dark sap out of the cracks and fissures now exposed.

The tree, rendered pale and naked and bleeding, shed its branches next. They fell to the ground like locks of hair, snipped by shears that were incredibly sharp. One of the branches rolled toward Eric after it crashed into the ground, and he stepped back.

The rest of the trees followed suit. An orchestra of ripping and tearing sounds filled the air at a deafening volume. Eric covered his ears and watched as the sap-blood poured out of the trees, spreading around them, soaking everything in its path. They shed their branches in unison, falling into the pooling blood. Great clouds of smoke issued forth as they drowned in the sap.

Eric understood then that it wasn't sap coming out from the trees but the same black smolder he had spent the night running from.

He also understood that the trees weren't really trees. They were fingers, slender and strong, that belonged to the humanoid shadow.

The smolder approached on the ground and the shadow approached from the sky. Eric backpedaled, trying to fight off the overwhelming sense of claustrophobia.

The burning smell of greenwood and grass mixed with the sulfur, but there was another scent that presented itself that Eric immediately recognized. Attached to the smell was a memory, a series of memories, each one a razor blade that cut him to the bone as they drew slowly through his mind.

The memory was of his first night with Monica, the intoxicating smell of her perfume as he kissed her neck. It was how her body felt under his hands, the sounds she made as they came together. It was also how the rush of air smelled as Monica pushed by him after their biggest fight more than a decade later when Eric found the evidence of her affair.

It wasn't just the smell of Monica's perfume; it was a cheater's perfume.

It was the smell of a million little lies that ruined a million little memories.

It was the way things smelled when good things went bad, like an apple left to rot on the ground. Instead of reminding him of all the pleasant memories he had associated with it, it would forever be a reminder of the failure of their marriage.

It was impossible that this particular smell would be here. Eric was trapped in this nightmare, brought on by his poorly thought-out and drunken idea to walk in the woods until he escaped the light that was the Hamilton skyline. Maybe he was having a stroke, or maybe the shock and fatigue and stress of this ordeal was causing him to hallucinate—

"Eric?"

He turned around in disbelief. There she was.

"Monica . . ." Eric managed to say, surprised and at a loss for words.

She stood before him at an arm's length, looking battered and beaten. It appeared she had had a night similar to his own. Clad in thin cotton shorts and a bloody sweatshirt, her face was bruised and sporting a split lip like she had gone a few rounds in a fistfight. Her hair was disheveled and pushed back from her face, strands of it stuck to her cheek with blood. She cradled her wrist, bruised and black and swollen, in the crook of her other arm.

"What's going—"

"How did you get—"

They spoke at the same time, both eager for explanations. There was a crashing sound from behind Eric that cut their conversation short. He turned back and saw that the Shadow Man was upon them.

It had the tops of the trees in its grip and was ripping them out of the ground. The trees pulled out of the earth, their roots dangling in the air like veins and dripping smolder that set the dry grass on fire. They swung up in the air, grotesque fingers at the end of the Shadow Man's phantom hands.

Monica grabbed Eric's hand and pulled him away.

Eric stumbled for a few steps, catching his balance

by putting his full weight on his damaged foot. He bit his tongue, drawing blood that he spat out. Monica pulled him along, not knowing of his injury. They ran ahead in the dry grass as far as they could manage until Eric dragged her to a stop. He fell first to his knees and then looked behind them to see where the Shadow Man was. It was still standing over where the cluster of trees had been, a hundred yards away at best. Eric collapsed to the ground and rolled onto his back.

"Are you okay?" Monica asked, leaning over him.

"I've been better," he replied. "What are you doing here? What happened to you?"

In defiance of the brevity of the situation, Monica looked like she was deciding if she wanted to tell Eric the truth or not. She looked ashamed.

"Trent beat me. Has been beating me for a while. It got really bad tonight, so I left."

Eric didn't respond. He pushed himself off the ground, afraid to let himself rest for too long.

"You left and you came here? To my house?"

"Yes, I thought—"

"You thought I would take you in?"

Monica raised a hand in protest. "I didn't know where else to go! I had to get out of there, Eric, he was going to kill me if I stayed. I couldn't go to any of my friends' houses like this. I just . . . I don't have anyone else."

Eric knew this wasn't the time or place for what he had to say, but the filter he typically employed that censored what he said aloud was gone. Somewhere along his way through the woods, he had lost it.

"You don't have me anymore, either."

He hated how much he enjoyed the look of shock on Monica's face.

"I know, but this is different, Eric. You have every right to be mad at me still. I fully admit that what I did was wrong, but I hoped that in my time of need—"

Eric laughed. "Your time of need? What, you thought that I'd take you in, give you a place to stay, protect you from the asshole you hooked up with? That you ended our marriage for?"

Monica began to cry. "I-I don't know. I guess I thought that you—"

"No, you didn't think about me. You thought about you. You thought about what *you* needed, what *you* thought you could get from me. And when you got what you needed, you'd leave me all over again."

She covered her mouth with her hand, shaking her head in disbelief. Monica sniffed and rubbed a tear from her cheek.

"I had no idea you were still so . . . angry."

18

Trent arrived at Eric's house not long after Monica had, as the hood of her car was still warm. The fact that all the lights were off made his anger and irritation flare up. He tried to keep his mind off of what that could mean and what could be happening somewhere inside.

It was dark out here, so far removed from the streetlamps of downtown Hamilton that he was used to. He thought about switching on the flashlight he took from his glove box, but he didn't want to lose the element of surprise. As it was, he had parked his truck a quarter mile down from the driveway, as he didn't want the sound of his loud exhaust to alert Monica and her ex-husband to his presence.

The cold air on his drive over and his walk to the house sobered him up. That was good because it allowed him to think clearly, but also bad because he was afraid that he might see what he had dreamed about being in those woods.

That's what the shotgun was for.

He bought the gun through a private sale brokered by a guy on the cleaning crew at work. Private sale meant there was no background check, which made it nearly untraceable. He kept it hidden underneath the passenger seat of his truck, loaded to capacity. The short barrel and the pistol grip made it easy to carry at the hip, and the sling made it easy to carry over his shoulder until he needed it. Trent had mounted a side saddle to the shotgun's receiver, which allowed him to carry an extra four shells. That gave him five shots of 2-ounce buck and four slugs. He would have felt more confident if he had his handgun on his hip, too, but he forgot that at his apartment.

Parking down the road turned out to be an unnecessary precaution. The front door had been locked, but he found the back door wide open. He let himself in, shotgun at the ready, but the first few rooms he checked were completely empty both of any furniture and belongings and of people. He tried a couple light switches, but there was no response. He chuckled wryly. The poor sap couldn't even afford his power bill.

Trent wandered through the house until he had cleared every room. The house was empty, so where was Monica's ex-husband? More importantly, where was Monica?

He recalled the conversation Monica had on the phone, where Eric admitted he was losing the house. Trent originally thought that was hilarious, but now that he saw the huge empty house, he thought it was almost sad. This house was so much nicer than his downtown apartment.

Trent went out through the back door and stood on the porch, his shotgun slung over his back. With no one home, he wasn't afraid now to use his flashlight. He clicked it on and swept it from left to right across the backyard, and spotted the trodden path in the overgrown grass.

So that's where they went.

He could almost picture it: Monica leading her ex-husband into the backyard for a midnight quickie under the stars. He happened to know by way of personal experience that Monica got a thrill from having sex in the outdoors.

Trent switched off the flashlight and brought the shotgun around to his chest. He slipped the flashlight into a clamp mounted on the forend, and with the pistol grip in one hand, he racked the forend to chamber one of the shells of buckshot. He smiled at the distinct sound it made.

The unkempt grass whispered against his legs as he walked through the backyard. His feet, cut and sore from walking on broken glass, were barely a thought. Trent focused on being as quiet as he could possibly be now that he was on the hunt.

He almost wanted to catch them in the act. He wanted to see the surprise on their faces when he came upon them. To see the surprise on their faces change into fear and pain when he released one round after another into their naked, whoring bodies. He was excited to find them because when he finally did, Trent knew he wouldn't have a problem pulling the trigger.

He knew because this wouldn't be the first time he killed someone. Hell, this wouldn't even be the second time.

Trent's father had been first.

His old man liked to drink, and when he got a little too far into his cups, he became someone else. It was a real-world Jekyll and Hyde situation. Trent's mother got the worst of it, and Trent hated seeing the bruises on her face and arms. Trent got his share of beatings from his father, but so long as he didn't ever touch his sister, he would accept every one of them.

Trent was fiercely protective of his sister. She was two years younger than him and embodied everything innocent and pure in a world that was often anything but. She believed the lies their mother told about where the bruises came from. Trent did everything he could to protect his sister from the evil side of their father so that she would stay innocent and pure for as long as she could.

Try as he might, Trent's efforts couldn't protect her all the time.

When Trent was fifteen, Trent awoke one night to the sound of a soft cry. He flew out of bed and down the hall to his sister's room. The door was closed, although she always slept with it open at least a crack. A pit formed in his stomach, and he braced himself for what he might see.

He tucked his shoulder and shoved open his sister's bedroom door. He saw his father standing over his sister's bed, his sister cowering in the corner, sheets and blankets drawn over herself in fear. His father, startled, took a step back.

"Trent, it's not what it looks like. I didn't touch her, I swear to God," he said quietly, his words mushing together. But Trent didn't hear him.

All he could hear was his sister's sniffling cries, and the only thing Trent could feel was his muscles twitching with adrenaline and rage.

The closest thing to hand was a belt. Trent grabbed it and whipped the end with the heavy clasp toward his father. It clocked him in the face and down he went, yelling obscenities and clutching his bleeding face. Trent went to his father on the floor and knelt.

"Why'd you do that?" Trent's father asked between cries. "I told you I didn't touch her."

"Was that because I interrupted you before you could?" Trent asked.

The moment of hesitation was all Trent needed.

He slipped the belt around his father's neck, pulling the tail end tightly through the buckle, wrapping it around a few more times for good measure. Trent stood up and dragged his father out of his sister's room by his neck. He dragged him down the hall and then down the stairs. His father's face was turning a deep red by the time Trent made it to the kitchen, and he had stopped clawing at his neck, had stopped making noises of any kind.

Trent brought his father out into their barn. Trent's father used it for working on the junk cars he often brought home to fix up and sell to support his drinking habit. He let go of the belt and let his father's head smack the hard-packed dirt floor.

His father's eyes fluttered open as Trent crouched down and passed the belt through itself to make a loop. He tried saying something to his son, but his weak voice couldn't be heard over the sound of dragging chains.

There was a chain hoist fastened to one of the beams of the barn. Trent's father had used it to lift engines and transmissions out of his junk cars to work on them, but not anymore. Trent secured the belt to the chain hoist's metal hook and, hand over hand, pulled on the chain and raised his father up off the ground by his neck.

He stood there for some time, watching his father soil himself as he died, not for a second regretting his choice or fearing the consequences.

"Wish you'd done that *before* he ruined her," he heard his mother say from behind him, taking Trent out of his reverie.

He turned to see his mother standing in the doorway of the barn, sporting a black eye that hadn't been there at dinner. Trent didn't want to believe what his mother was saying.

"You knew he was . . ." He couldn't bring himself to say the words out loud.

Trent's mother shrugged her shoulders.

"It was only a matter of time before he got sick of me," she said. "Better her than—"

Trent couldn't remember what happened next. It was the first time he blacked out from anger, but it wouldn't be the last. All he knew was that when he came down off the anger high, both his parents were hanging from the hoist, a knife plunged to the hilt into his mother's chest. The sound of blood pattering on the dirt floor and clinking chains filtered in over the sound of his heartbeat in his ears.

His sister found him in the barn, watching their parents swing from the hoist. Trent had done what he felt was necessary to protect his sister but instead of being grateful, his sister became terrified of what Trent had become. She cowered from him, her expression matching the way she looked when Trent had caught their father in her bedroom.

She ran inside and barricaded herself in her room. Trent followed, kneeling outside her door, pleading for her to let him in. She refused, and Trent eventually fell asleep on her doorstep. She was gone when he woke, and he never saw her again.

The events of that night shaped his psyche, putting him on a path to violent, self-destructive behavior that made him more like his father than he would ever admit. It's what led him to be where he was right now: walking through tall grass, hunting for his cheating girlfriend.

He was so confident that he'd find Monica and Eric in the grass that he forgot about what he had seen in the woods the last time he was here. He forgot about the vision of the man with the empty chest, soul-steam pouring out.

Trent clicked the safety off on his shotgun.

Given the traumatic story that was his childhood,

even as righteous as his actions might have been on principle, Trent was confident that he'd have no qualms with blasting holes into his girlfriend and her ex-husband.

He might even be looking forward to it.

19

"You had no idea? What part of my behavior told you otherwise?"

Monica stood with one knee popped forward, a classic Monica pose that told Eric she was digging in her heels, intending to win this argument. Over the course of their relationship, she had easily won most of their arguments, a fact she often reminded him of. Some were won fair and square, but some because Eric just didn't care enough to keep asserting his point.

"You've got to be kidding me. Eric, you are one of the most guarded people I've ever met!"

She was right, but Eric wasn't going to give her the satisfaction of admitting that. He was guarded, but if he was truly honest with himself, he was angry more than anything else. Managing his anger had been a long-standing problem, beginning when he was a child. He had an explosive temper, and his parents tried to help him control it. Their advice, while well-intentioned, was less about how to manage the anger and have a proportional response to things than it was about how to just not express it at all.

He was made to feel like his anger was a noxious

substance, his own personal Chernobyl, to be handled at arm's length in a rubber hazmat suit. It was better for everyone if he just locked it all away, buried it deep instead of having to clean up the fallout. By the time he was an adolescent, Eric had learned to suppress it completely.

He would come to understand that suppressed anger was the most dangerous kind.

It was a powder keg, and a single spark was all that was needed to set it off. Years of suppressed emotions and repressed feelings were pushed down and ignored under the promise of dealing with it later, but later never came. It was a toxic thing to do with such a strong emotion, but suppressing anger was the only way Eric knew how to keep from losing it completely.

He became quite good at it.

And so what if he was guarded? At least he had been a devoted spouse. If there was ever a time to be angry, to express the emotion he rarely ever let out of its cage, it was now. It was justifiable, and some might say he had even earned it.

Eric unleashed it all.

His anger poured out of him through his words, heavy with the vitriol he had carried within him for decades, long before he met Monica. It didn't matter that some of it was misplaced. He laid it all on her. With every word he spoke, the angrier he became. It was a fire that fed itself, and he was an inferno before he was half done.

When he was done, he couldn't remember most of what he said. He could feel his words lingering in the air like smoke, and he could see surprise and pain on Monica's face.

Eric didn't care how Monica felt. He felt unburdened for the first time since he was a child, like he had finally exhaled the toxic breath he had been holding in for far too long. Iron bars had been wrapped around his chest and the lock that held them together was now broken. He breathed in what felt like his first true deep breath.

He took a perverse sense of pleasure in seeing the effect his words had on Monica. He waited for her to respond, but instead of a response, her expression turned from that of shock and surprise to absolute terror. Her eyes shifted to something behind him, and Eric turned around to see what caught her attention.

It was the Shadow Man, and it grabbed for Eric with its tree-trunk fingers. The roots of the trees unfurled, reaching out for him like tentacles. The smolder Eric found crawling on him became a surging, searing heat that laced up his leg. His sneaker melted, the canvas shriveling up and peeling away from the rubber sole that turned into a puddle underneath his foot. It melted his skin as he sunk down into the molten rubber, and Eric was rendered breathless from the pain.

The denim of his jeans caught fire from the intense heat. Eric dropped to the ground and rolled, praying that the grass would put out the flames and not catch on fire, too. He covered his face with his hands as he rolled and had the absurd thought to be thankful he learned the 'stop-drop-roll' lesson in kindergarten.

Monica found her voice and started screaming. She ran after Eric, stripping out of her sweatshirt. The thick scab that had formed into the fabric from the slash on her back tore off, and Monica felt fresh blood trickle down her back. She grabbed hold of the sweatshirt with both hands, feeling the broken bones splinter in her swollen wrist, and beat at the flames covering Eric's legs. She gagged from the smell of burning flesh and hot rubber that filled her nose, and at last, the flames sputtered out.

Monica tossed her sweatshirt aside and knelt down next to Eric. He was on his stomach, and Monica rolled him over onto his back to see if he was still conscious. She focused on his face, not wanting to see the damage the fire had done to his legs.

"Eric, you need to breathe," she said, forcing her voice to be calm.

As if he had forgotten, Eric gasped in a ragged breath.

He did a quick self-assessment, and oddly enough, he was not in any pain. Something had happened when he fell to the ground. There was a crack in his back, and then a flash that exploded in his skull. After that, everything went numb from his waist down. Eric was dazed but understood what that meant. He was sure he'd feel different about it later, but as he surveyed his horribly burned legs, he considered it another blessing in disguise.

"I'm okay," Eric said. "I think . . . I think something in my back is broken. I can't feel my legs."

"What? How?"

There wasn't enough time to get into that. Whether it was the Shadow Man or the smolder, Eric was beginning to feel like a wounded mouse being played with by a housecat, and he was getting quite sick of it. He used his arms to push himself up to a seated position and Monica grabbed onto one of his hands to help him.

"That doesn't matter. We just need to get out of here."

Monica pulled Eric in closer to her and wrapped her arms around him in a tight embrace, sobbing.

"I'm so scared, Eric. What is this place?"

Eric sighed. "I don't know."

He closed his eyes, trying hard not to breathe her perfume. He didn't want this moment to become another painful memory associated with it. He had too many already.

With Eric's eyes closed and Monica's back turned, they both failed to see that someone had joined them in the Clearing.

"I *fucking* knew it."

Monica's body tensed instantly. Eric's eyes flew open, and across the field, he saw, inexplicably, Trent. His ex-wife's asshole boyfriend.

Monica let go of Eric and stood up. The look of fear and defeat on her face was heartbreaking, and as much as Eric had been angry at Monica for how she had completely upended his life, he became even angrier at Trent. Monica stood in front of Eric like a shield, facing Trent head-on.

"Trent, it's not what you think. There's—"

A thundercloud detonated, and Monica's back exploded.

Eric felt something hot and stringy spatter across his face and chest, some getting into his eyes and mouth. Monica collapsed backward onto the grass and Eric saw the holes in her chest, blood seeping out of them, and knew she would soon be dead.

Eric looked up and saw Trent, a short-barreled

shotgun at his hip. Tendrils of smoke rose out of the barrel and he wore a smug smile on his face.

"You just couldn't keep it in your pants, could you, Mon?" he asked.

"You've got it all wrong, Trent. Nothing happened," Eric replied, forcing himself to remain calm.

"Says the guy whose hands were all over her ass just a few seconds ago." Trent racked back the pump action of his shotgun and it spit out the used shell that had been fired into Monica. Eric started to protest further, but Trent chambered another round and aimed the shotgun at Eric's face. "Do me a favor and just shut the hell up. I know what I saw."

A gurgling came from Monica's throat as she choked on her own blood. As much as Eric had grown to hate her for the mistakes she made, she didn't deserve an ending like this. He hated that there was nothing he could do except watch her bleed out in front of him.

Trent dipped the barrel down toward the ground and walked up to Eric. The gurgling in Monica's throat turned into a slow hiss, and then nothing. Her eyes rolled back to all whites. She was dead.

Eric focused his mind on trying to get his legs to move. He willed his nerves to light back up, but there was nothing but static. As Trent approached, he looked at Eric's legs with disgust.

"What happened to your legs?" Trent asked. "They look a little crispy."

"That tends to happen around here. You should be careful," Eric replied.

"You're the one who should have been careful."

The big show of bravado that Eric had seen when Monica moved out was back. Chest puffed out, wide-legged stance, and an expression that was excessively grim and serious. Eric knew this was meant to intimidate, but Eric found it amusing. Eric looked away, and when Trent stopped in front of Eric, he squatted so they were face to face.

"You shouldn't have been messing around with another man's woman," Trent said. "Bad things tend to happen when you start to fuck around with something that's not yours. People get hurt."

Eric stifled a chuckle, disguising it as a cough, and hid his smile under his hand. "You really should take some of your own advice. You fucked around with another man's woman and now look what's happened."

Trent looked surprised at his own hypocrisy and then at Monica's corpse on the ground next to him. He cleared his throat. "Consider that a promise fulfilled. Bitch had it coming. Once a cheater, always a cheater."

He tucked the barrel of his shotgun underneath Eric's chin. The barrel was warm and smelled of gunpowder and oil.

"And I think it's best that you take this conversation seriously. I don't take kindly to being laughed at."

Eric looked down the barrel at Trent's hand and saw his finger wrapped around the trigger.

"Sure thing," he agreed instinctively. "I don't want any trouble."

"Good," Trent said. He looked happy to be in control, to have the upper hand.

Eric seemed to know one thing that Trent

apparently did not: The Shadow Man was upon them. Eric could see the smolder spreading across the grass. They did not have the luxury of time for the evil villain monologue before Trent decided if he was going to shoot Eric or not.

"I always suspected you two were still fucking," Trent said. "I just never had the proof until now. That's why she came down with that case of lead poisoning. No one cheats on me and gets away with it."

It was an outlandish statement, a baseless accusation with no evidence other than an insecure man's wild imagination, but it gave Eric an idea.

"Well, it's like you said. Once a cheater, always a cheater."

Readjusting his grip on the trigger, Trent nodded and looked over at Monica's body. Congealing blood had pooled into her navel.

"But I suppose you really can't blame her too much," Eric continued.

Trent's eyes snapped back to Eric. "What do you mean?"

"Well, it can be difficult to satisfy a woman the right way. Some men just don't have the right equipment."

The color in Trent's face went from white to deep red. Eric kept an eye on his trigger finger and watched it bear down.

"Fuck you, you fucking pri—"

Eric quickly ducked to one side and out of the way of the shotgun barrel. As he fell, Eric pushed the forend of the gun back toward Trent then rolled away. The commotion caused Trent to lose his balance, and he leaned forward to avoid tumbling over, he put his own face in front of the barrel.

The shotgun discharged as Eric rolled away, another explosively loud blast that made Eric's ears ring. Trent fell backward to the ground, dropping the gun. He howled and screamed, a grating noise that did not at all sound human.

Eric stopped rolling and looked over to where Trent lay clutching his face, writhing in pain. His screaming descended into a moan and then to silence. Eric thought Trent was dead until he stood up.

Trent's face was a horrific display, a large section of it blown off by the shotgun blast. The point-blank shot had torn off the left side from his chin to his ear. Blood and a thick, viscous fluid drained from the cavity, his shattered lower jaw drooping down from the side still connected to his skull.

Inexplicably, Trent tried to speak. He only succeeded in separating the intact portion of his jaw from the rest of his face. It swung down, dangling from skin and muscle tissue. A thick chunk of tissue fell to the ground, which Eric recognized as Trent's tongue. Trent moaned from deep within his throat, blood sputtering out of the space where his mouth used to be.

He leaned down to the ground and picked up his shotgun.

Eric was stunned, unsure how Trent was able to stay on his feet. If the injury itself didn't slow him, surely the blood loss would have weakened him. Freshets of blood issued out of the crescent-shaped wound. Eric remembered back to a week he had spent on his uncle's chicken farm one summer when he was eight or nine years old. He had watched his uncle slaughter a rooster that had become aggressive. One swift chop of the hatchet was all it took to cut off the rooster's head, and Eric looked on in horror and disgust as the rooster ran around the yard, headless.

Trent was clearly struggling, his fingers not having the same dexterity as he tried to properly grip the shotgun. He grabbed the pistol grip and dropped the forend into the crook of his arm. Trent pushed forward on the grip and the slide pushed back, ejecting the empty shell. With the chamber empty, he lifted the barrel toward the sky and placed his hand around the forend. He let go of the pistol grip and the weight of the gun pulled downward on the slide, racking another shell into position.

Slowly and deliberately, Trent leveled the barrel at Eric.

Eric closed his eyes, wondering if he'd hear the sound of the gun before he died. He didn't know what was faster; the speed of sound or a load of buckshot. He waited for what seemed like an eternity, but nothing happened. He opened his eyes just a crack.

Trent was still standing there, aiming the shotgun at Eric's chest. He was swaying on his feet and looked like he was going to expire at any moment. Eric glanced down at Trent's index finger wrapped tightly around the trigger, a hair's breadth away from firing. His eyes were glassed over and pointed in different directions, and it looked like a lobe of his brain was drooping out from his open skull.

Behind Trent was the Shadow Man.

20

The Nothing had started its hunt with only one prey to track and catch but had somehow wound up with three. It was not sure where the other two had come from, but one of them was dead now. The dead had no value to the Nothing because what it harvested from the humans could only be taken while they were alive:

Anger.

Powerful and seductive and ripe with unpredictable strength, the Nothing lived for anger. It *was* anger in a physical form, or at least as much a physical presence as it could muster. Anger gave the Nothing a sort of static, an energy that allowed the Nothing to exist. The more anger it collected, the stronger the Nothing became.

The Nothing had been collecting anger for a very long time. It had become quite strong, strong enough to destroy an entire forest to collect from one man who had more anger within him than anyone else it had encountered.

The man it had been chasing through the woods was quite special. He had anger in such high quantity that it was difficult for the Nothing exercise restraint. It wanted nothing more than to swoop in and drink him dry. Instead, the Nothing had let the man wander through its woods for hours, knowing that getting lost often made humans quite frustrated, and frustration paved the way for anger.

But then the man with the thunder came. He had anger and lots of it, but it was dirty. Tainted. The Nothing didn't want what that man had to offer. He was like a murky, stagnant pool.

The Nothing knew what the thunder was. The thunder killed things; it had seen many men with thunder in its woods, had seen the many deer slaughtered by it.

Some of those men had made it out of the woods with their kill. They did not have what the Nothing wanted, at least not enough of it to make the effort worth it. The rest had been taken and returned to the ground, and the Nothing's strength grew.

The thunder cracked a second time, and there was a shift in the new man's scent. His anger was gone, wholly replaced by fear.

That gave the Nothing pause, as true and proper fear was like a filter. Fear clarified everything, and it made the man with the thunder's murky anger instantly clear. It separated any of the other emotions that are related to anger by a variety of tangents, making the Nothing's job incredibly easy. The Nothing shifted its focus away from the man it had been chasing, having made up its mind.

The man with the thunder would go first.

21

A cough shook a shower of blood out of Trent's throat, a glut of blood landing on Monica's ashen face.

Faced with both the shotgun aimed at his gut and the Shadow Man, Eric wasn't sure what would be the end of him. Like the batteries in his flashlight, like the unsteadiness in his stomach, he knew he was just biding his time until it was over. Until everything was over.

Eric looked down at his ruined legs. They were blackened and stiff, and if he somehow survived this night and made it to a hospital, he fully expected that he'd lose both of them at the waist.

He regretted the stupidity of his idea to go for that damn walk. It was foolish to think that he'd be able to escape the brightness he saw on the skyline. He was so angry at that light, wanting so much to be immersed in darkness that he sought his solace in the woods.

Was it the light he was angry at or was it what he thought the light represented?

Or had he been shithouse drunk and just pissed off at the whole goddamn world?

Eric looked up and saw the spreading smolder had blackened the entire Clearing. There was nothing but charred grass except for the shrinking plot he lay on, that he shared with Trent and Monica. It had already started to grow like death moss on Monica, starting at her feet and working its way up her legs. Soon, it would cover her completely, and she would disappear forever.

It was spreading faster now, coming in like the rising tide. Eric heard a dry snapping sound from behind him and turned at the waist to see that the smolder had continued to spread through the woods behind him and was now passing the tree line. It was closing in on him from all directions.

So, this was it.

The ordeal he put himself in was going to be over soon.

A small spark ignited deep in Eric's brain. It traveled along a fuse line of synapses that set off a chain reaction in his mind.

The Clearing plunged into complete darkness as Eric went blind.

22

At the same time that the world around Eric went dark, the shotgun slipped out of Trent's weakened hands.

The barrel jackknifed toward Trent when the pistol grip came into contact with the ground. The shotgun discharged on impact and a load of buckshot went into his chest.

Eric heard the gun go off and winced, expecting to feel the lead pellets tear through his body, but nothing happened. The gunshot echoed across the Clearing and Eric was still alive. He was breathless but elated.

As he searched through his blindness to see something, anything, Eric realized he could still see, except the only thing he saw was the Shadow Man.

No, it wasn't called the Shadow Man. Eric had subconsciously given the shadow a name as an automatic response to identify with what had been chasing him. But now that he could see it, now that he was on the same level as it, he knew what its real name was as if the knowledge had just been planted in his brain.

It was Nothing.

The Nothing hovered just above the ground on a rolling fog. The trees it had uprooted to use as hands had become the skeleton that gave it the humanoid shape reminiscent of Tolkien's Ents, with a grotesque skull made of misshapen knots and burls. A series of spines rose off of its backbone, and small offshoots of splintering branches grew nearly everywhere.

Two large, curved branches, thick like tusks, grew out of where its eyes should have been. The tusks ended in sharp points that looked like they had been whittled down.

A tangle of roots spread forth from its hands. The roots stretched out and wrapped around a blank human shape that Eric knew to be Trent. He was glad he was seeing this part with his mind instead of his eyes because the sound of what the Nothing did to Trent to consume him was horrible enough.

Eric heard the sound of Trent's arms being pulled out of their sockets, muscles separating, tendons snapping. There was the wet spray of his blood as it hit the grass, followed by the crunch of his bones as they were ground into dust. All of that was buried under the sound of Trent screaming, bellowing in agony as he was stripped of his life. It was an awful terror of noise, and Eric covered his ears though he knew it would do no good.

When the Nothing ripped out Trent's throat, the screaming abruptly stopped, leaving behind an echo that rippled back across the open Clearing. The Nothing drank from him, and when it finished, threw Trent's body aside.

Trent's body landed somewhere in the darkness that surrounded them, where the smolder took the rest.

Monica's corpse was slowly disappearing. Eric could see the shape of her body flattening like a deflating balloon underneath the smolder. After hearing what had become of Trent, he was glad she had been spared the same fate.

Eric felt something sliding up his back. He knew by the cool, intense heat he felt that it was the smolder. He knew it was coming, knew it was inevitable. It spread over him like a second skin, covering his face and sliding down his throat. He considered the possibility that he might be hallucinating, but it felt too real.

In a way that unsettled him, it felt familiar, an intensely lucid déjà vu.

Underneath the smolder, Eric thought he would burn. He had seen it turn everything it touched to ash within an instant and had lost some of his own toes to it. He was confused as to why he wasn't burning alive, disappearing into the ground like Trent, like Monica, like the doe.

He had barely finished the thought when he felt something like a knife blade run down his legs. His legs came alive with such incredible pain that it laid him out flat on the ground, thrashing violently in a seizure. The pain wasn't just in his legs now: It was *everywhere.*

The smolder inched down his throat and reached his stomach, blooming outward. Every bone in his body felt like it was being scraped clean with razor blades, the marrow inside being replaced with barbed wire. The cartilage in his joints melted away. The only part of Eric that caught on fire, however briefly, was his hair. Every follicle lit up and burnt each individual strand of hair in a flash.

A layer of scales grew over Eric's bones. The scales expanded and hardened, layering upon themselves until he was covered in them, thick like armor. As he suffocated under the weight of the scales, the nerves in his entire body went electric, lighting up in Eric's brain like runway lights. And just as quick as it began, the pain switched off. The memory of it hung in the air like a foul smell.

Eric, still flat on his back, felt the presence of the Nothing loom over him. He felt the undulating waves of smolder that were drowning him. The riptide that pulled him under was strong, a thick atmosphere that filled his lungs without mercy.

Except he didn't have lungs. Not anymore.

The pressure he felt was the absence of breathing, no longer necessary because his chest was a hollow trunk. The pressure was the scales tightening, securing themselves in place.

Eric rolled to one side and pushed himself off the ground. As he stood up, he saw how his body had been changed by the smolder. Gone were his arms and legs. Gone was every scrap of flesh. Gone were the things that made him human, as everything he was had been replaced with the wooden skeleton made up of the trees that lived in the Clearing.

The only thing left that had not yet been transformed was his skull.

Eric blinked his mind's eye, and suddenly, he was watching himself from the Nothing's eyes. He saw firsthand how his skull flowered from within. It peeled up and out in jagged strips, exposing his brain pulsating in the dark. Eric felt something inside the Nothing surge and knew it to be hunger.

The Nothing spoke to Eric, using images instead of

words.

It showed him what it wanted from him.

Inside Eric's brain, there was something much darker than the smolder that enveloped him. It traced between the folds and curves, a liquid in which his brain tissue steeped. Its origin was deep within his brain, near the stem. It was a narrow but deep well into the part of his soul that was hidden from everyone. The epicenter where all of the darkness that was inside of him started.

The darkness was anger.

He blinked again and switched out of the Nothing's eyes and back to his own. He saw the long, spindly roots of the Nothing's hands reach out toward him. They were needle-sharp, ready to pierce deep into his brain to take what it hungered for. Eric tried to move away but couldn't. He was anchored to the smolder, caught in the web of the spider that had been chasing him the entire night.

A shiver of fear raced through him, and with it came the clarity of realizing something about himself that he had not known. Eric realized the true danger of what he had kept buried inside of him for so long.

The roots of his anger were incredibly deep. It began in his youth when he suffered an injury that did not damage his flesh but his psyche. That wound would never heal, scabbing and tearing open over and over again throughout the decades that passed until it was a festering sore, perpetually broken. In defiance of that weakness, it was a source of incredible strength, but one that he had been taught to suppress and ignore. He had briefly tapped into it earlier, but Eric knew now that he had barely scratched the surface.

The Nothing's needle fingers pierced into the tissue of Eric's brain. He knew that the Nothing wanted to drain him of his anger, to soak up every single atom of it and let the smolder take him. Anger is what made the Nothing stronger, and Eric was a source of it unlike any other. Eric felt the needles push through the tissue, separating the lobes, pushing his gray matter aside to expose the darkened core it wanted so desperately.

Eric could sense the Nothing's eagerness to consume him. It was so focused on its solitary goal, the culmination of all its efforts on this night, that it was not capable of any other thought.

The Nothing's needle fingers reached Eric's amygdala. It paused for just a moment to admire the savage beauty of it. The raw energy it contained, the incredible potential was far more than it had imagined or hoped for.

But something was wrong.

A ripple appeared in the pool of anger, as if something was coming up from underneath the surface.

A thick vine shot through the surface, coming from the stem of Eric's brain and splitting out into multiple smaller fibrous strands. Each one grabbed hold of the Nothing's needle fingers and shattered them easily, breaking them off like dry branches on a dead tree before it could so much as sample the vintage of Eric's anger. The vine latched onto the Nothing and pushed back, continued to grow and extend upward, curving out of Eric's skull like a scorpion tail.

It grew within Eric as well. It threaded itself through his arms and legs, breaking him free of his restraints caused by the smolder. Eric felt himself stretching, growing taller, thicker, and stronger. The pool of anger inside his brain surged like an ocean in a hurricane, great waves of black crashing up against the confines of his brain, each one more violent than the last, until it poured out of him.

Eric reached out with his hands to grab hold of the Nothing. He towered over it now, dominating the Clearing with his stature. He grasped onto the Nothing's tusks with each hand and pulled down, bringing it to its knees. The Nothing tried to fight back, tried to push his hands away with its tree-trunk arms, tried to use the smolder to burn him, anything to escape Eric's grasp.

A flurry of images passed through Eric's mind. He saw flashes of all the times the Nothing had set its trap, saw the bodies of the nameless people who had been lured into the Clearing for the sake of satiating the Nothing's appetite. He saw every single person's final moment before they were cracked open, the worst and angriest parts of their souls consumed, their empty shells discarded and turned to ash.

Eric also saw that it was tied to this place. Where he stood, using his newfound strength to hold down the beast, was the site of the Nothing's creation. Time before time, it came to exist and poisoned the soil until the Nothing was the only thing that could grow. It could not leave this place, but it could use its immense power to draw that which is sought into its trap.

It had been immensely successful, but Eric did not intend to let it continue any further.

Whatever connected Eric to the Nothing allowed the Nothing to know Eric's choice and it began to thrash from side to side, trying to break free from his grasp. It was a wasted effort, as the darkness that Eric finally allowed himself to harness was far stronger than the total amount the Nothing had accumulated over the centuries of its existence.

With nearly no effort, Eric lifted the Nothing up off the ground by its tusks. The Nothing was soaked with the darkness that had been pouring out of Eric's brain. It was a darkness that only he could use that issued from his soul like a fountain, flooding the open field. Eric lifted the Nothing until he was face to face with it.

He pulled apart the Nothing's skull. It split open noisily, its burls and knots cracking wide to reveal a cavity that reeked of rot and malice. Inside this space were two brightly burning spheres, sputtering and swirling like balls of gas. Eric thought they looked like stars, beautiful and foreign, and briefly admired them before he tore them out and tossed them aside. They sizzled and went dark as they sunk into the smolder that had risen around them.

With the Nothing's skull splayed open, the two halves lying flat like a book at the top of the Nothing's thick neck, Eric snapped off the ends of the Nothing's tusks. He released his grip, the scorpion vine that had grown out of his brain coiling neatly back. The Nothing tumbled down, splashing into the smolder.

Eric knew, in the same way he knew the Nothing's name, that the heart of the Nothing was inside the gaping maw between the halves of its skull. Somewhere down inside there, he would find the only way to extinguish the Nothing's fire forever, putting an end to its reign. The smolder was ineffective against the Nothing. Instead of turning to ash like everything else it touched, the Nothing floated on the surface like driftwood.

The scorpion vine launched itself toward the Nothing's heart. It plunged into the opening between the halves of its gutted skull, disappearing into the void. In the moments that passed, while he waited for it to reach the heart, Eric became overwhelmed with a staggering amount of dread.

He shouldn't have tried to fight back.

This had all been a grave mistake.

It was too late.

It was another trap that Eric failed to see, and now, he was fully ensnared.

23

The splayed parts of the Nothing's skull flared open even further, stretching and flowering out to become the hungry mouth that Eric had likened it to just moments earlier. The ocean of darkness that had been flooding the field drained into the Nothing's mouth like a storm drain, swirling around Eric's feet, throwing him off balance. Something unseen under the surface wrapped itself around his legs, pulling him under, and Eric was helpless to stop it.

When Eric surfaced, there was a storm raging all around him. It was a tempest of souls, the energy of those who had the worst parts of them taken by the Nothing built up into a thundercloud of unadulterated anger and evil.

Thunder rolled, lightning arced, and black rain fell in sheets. He looked up at the thunderheads above and around him, and saw the depths of the anger in the souls the Nothing had collected.

Instinct told Eric that this was the end. There was no escaping this place, the final resting place for everything that the Nothing hoarded to make itself stronger.

Eric wanted so badly to give up. Hadn't he suffered enough on this night, the longest of any in his life? If this really was the end of the line, then let's get it over with already. It seemed that the Nothing wanted something more from him, and was deriving some sick pleasure from dragging it out of him ever so slowly.

The roots that had dragged him into this place were wrapped firmly around his legs but were making their way up his thighs, strong enough to make Eric wish he hadn't regained use of them. Something dug painfully into his hip, like something hard had become trapped under the scales that had replaced his flesh.

It was the pocketknife he had salvaged from that moldy backpack.

Eric grabbed for it, peeling apart the scales, breaking them off so that he could take the knife out from underneath. When he pulled it out, he held it in front of his face like it was a trophy, and unfolded the blade. It locked open with a secure click.

It was an expensive blade, sharp and with serrations that looked hungry and eager to cut. He wasn't sure how effective it would be against the Nothing. Eric thought he knew what would destroy it, but he had been wrong.

It seemed like death was the only way out.

. . . and maybe that was it.

Eric took the tip of the blade and jabbed it into his chest. It sunk into one of the scales nearly an inch and then stopped. He pushed down on the handle of the knife, prying the scale up. It chipped off, and when Eric looked down to see what had been left behind, he saw his heart pumping underneath his sternum.

He knew if he hesitated, he would never do it. In some ways, Eric knew this would be the way the night would end. He wasn't sure why he had tried to get ahead of his fate, to try to change it. Survival instinct, he supposed, but he was tired.

The knife cut neatly into the tough muscle of his heart. He almost didn't feel it, at least not at first. It began as a warm sting but when the serrations dug in, it took his breath away. Eric plunged the blade in as far as it would go, and then pulled it back out. Eric's broken heart pumped only a few more beats before stopping. A steady stream of blood poured out of the hole he had cut, washing away in the black rainwater.

One by one, the scales that had grown over Eric's body fell off. They fell into the blackwater and wriggled away under the surface like they were leeches that had had their fill and were off in search of a new victim. The vines that had been wrapping around his legs released as well, and Eric felt the scorpion vine that grew out of his skull detach. It tumbled off his shoulders, landing in the blackwater among the scales that were still fleeing his body.

Eric was free, but he was bleeding out. He knelt down, feeling his knees becoming weak.

He fell to his knees, blackness starting to creep in around the corners of his vision.

"Eric?" a voice called out from far away.

A familiar smell attached to a painful memory.

"Monica?" he replied.

She stepped out of a heavy fog that had collected around him, smiling and healed. Eric knew it was a hallucination, but he wanted it to be real, and he figured he had been through enough on this night to allow himself the delusion. He didn't want to be alone when he died, much less alone inside a monster's belly.

"What are you doing here?" he asked, breathless, confused.

Monica did not respond, staying silent until she was close to him. She knelt down in the black water like she was unaware it was even there. Thunder crashed and lightning cracked above them, but she didn't flinch a single time. Instead, her smile, bright and happy, deepened as she looked at him. She took his hand and then looked around her at the expanse of the storm that surrounded them.

"Look at the size of this place!" she said at last. "You could yell at the top of your lungs and no one would be close enough to hear it."

Eric smiled wistfully, the irony painfully obvious. "That's kind of the point."

"Where are we?" she asked.

"We're in the belly of the beast."

A tightness spread across Eric's chest and he began to spasm. Monica placed her hand on his heart, blood still feebly pumping out of the hole he'd cut.

"How'd you wind up here?"

Eric managed a short laugh.

"I was . . . trying to get away from you."

She laughed and looked up at the sky. "Guess that didn't work out too well for you, did it?"

Her hair fell around her shoulders, and Eric was struck by how beautiful she was. When she looked back down at him, her expression was like it had been before, when things were still good between them . . . before she found someone else to look at that way.

"What'd I do wrong?" Eric asked. "And why Trent?"

Monica sighed. "It was never anything you did, Eric. We were never going to be together forever. You had to have felt that, too. I don't think I was the only one."

She spoke as if it was obvious he felt the same way, when he felt the polar opposite.

"No. When I said my vows at our wedding, I meant it when I said 'til death do us part.' You're telling me you didn't?"

She took her hand off his heart and wiped her cheek. His blood, bright red, stained her hand and streaked across the pale white of her skin.

"No," she said. "You were . . ."

Eric felt tears streaming down his face. "What? A chump?"

"You were *safe*."

He let himself fall to the side, getting off of his knees and sitting with his legs kicked out to one side.

"You were a good guy, Eric! A decent man who loved me and wanted to marry me. You didn't have a mean bone in your body, so I knew you'd never do anything to hurt me. I—"

"You thought you'd hurt me, instead? By lying to me for ten years? For wasting a decade of my life?" Eric tried to raise his voice but found it was hard to catch his breath.

A tear traced down Monica's cheek now. It was black and left behind a river of soot as it cut through the streak of blood on her face.

"Eric, I'm—"

"No, I'm done listening to you."

He closed his eyes and pushed her away.

"Eric?"

Monica's voice sounded scared, the way she used to sound that would make him drop everything and run to her side.

Not anymore.

He was angry, so very angry to be forced to admit the truth to himself. One that he had known but denied since the day of their wedding. He had known she didn't love him the way he loved her. He had the foolish hope, standing there at the altar, that this was something that would change over time.

Forgetting she was an illusion, he wished she was still dead, and that she hadn't somehow come back to remind him of the truth.

Denial was so much easier to handle.

He didn't want to participate in this hallucination any longer but didn't think he'd have to. Based on how weak he felt, he didn't think he had much time left.

"Eric!" she screamed.

Instinctively, Eric's eyes snapped open and he saw

Monica floating in the air above him, suspended from her neck by a thick root that came down from the thundercloud overhead.

He stared at her, helpless to do anything. If he was being honest with himself (better late than never), he wasn't sure that he wanted to help her even if he could.

She whimpered as her bottom lip split open and she spit out blood. She screamed and arched her back, and Eric heard the sound of tearing skin as her back was slashed open.

A crash of thunder just overhead rang out, except Eric knew it wasn't thunder. A patchwork pattern of blood appeared on her chest and stomach as shotgun pellets perforated her torso. She grunted with the impact, and then, before he could so much as blink, her face disappeared as the second round slammed into her.

Monica went limp, and the root that had been wrapped around her neck released her. Her body turned to ash as it fell, catching on the wind that swirled and swelled with the storm.

Eric felt a pang of guilt before remembering it was all a hallucination. It had been a lucid dream, incredibly vivid as his own death approached.

He had wished her dead, and now, she was.

He fell back into the water, sinking below the surface.

I wish I was dead, too.

/////

Eric sunk to the bottom. He was tossed and pushed around by the waves, but the water calmed the further he sunk.

Tall grass, coarse and slimy, brushed against his skin, reminding him of a cat's tongue. He nestled into it as he came to rest on the bottom where everything was still and quiet.

It was dark and Eric was tired. So tired that he wanted to cry from the incapacitating fatigue he felt in every cell of his body. He wanted to close his eyes, knowing that if he fell asleep, he would not wake up.

He closed them anyway.

Fucking Monica.

Eric dreamed.

He dreamed he was a river, and there were many brooks, creeks, and streams that emptied into him. His reach was massive, spreading out over an immense distance, and his current was strong, dangerous, and endless. His current raged when it rained, babbled when there was a drought. He eroded the land, carving his way through rock and sand alike, an unstoppable force.

The current flowed eternal, always moving, always carrying something away with it.

There was a body.

It floated facedown, tossed and pushed around by the will of the water until the river reached a point where moving forward became impossible.

The dam was infinite, stretching up into the sky, into the clouds. It encircled the earth, and for the first time ever, there was no place for the river to go. Its raging waters surged against the impassable wall, trying its hardest to find even the smallest of cracks.

But there were none.

The body, content to keep floating, rode on the surface of the water and slammed into the dam. Its skull cracked against it and split open, letting out a slurry of its brains, which the river water promptly washed away.

The water, having found a new space to occupy, filled the empty skull.

It found that it wasn't just a skull, but a drain to somewhere else.

More and more water rushed in to replace the water that disappeared into the head of the body floating in the river. The river emptied itself into the body until there was no water left. With not a drop of water anywhere, the sun dried up the riverbed.

The body, the dead man, sat leaning against the dam as if he had fallen asleep. His bloated and waterlogged skin shriveled in the heat of the sun, turning to leather and causing his posture to change.

The man fell over and he, never having been dead in the first place, woke up.

His skull, misshapen from breaking open against the dam, scraped against the dam as he stood. The jagged parts of the skull tore through the dam, and it began to crumble.

He stood back, watching the dam collapse in front of him. He felt the strength of the river within him, the sheer power of it incomprehensible.

An opening appeared in the dam, big enough to allow the man to pass through.

The man walked carefully on the rubble toward the opening.

There was only a void on the other side, and so dark that he couldn't see anything. The man wasn't sure if he wanted to proceed any further, but the crumbling ground underfoot decided for him.

He lost his footing and fell into

/////

the nothing.

Eric woke up with a start, gasping for breath.

Rough grass scraped against his skin as he sat up, thrashing around in the dark water.

No, the dark water was gone. The storm of angry souls was gone, the Clearing was gone.

He got to his knees and collected his bearings. Eric thought—

NO.

A door in his brain slammed closed.

NO, it said. *NO.*

He wasn't Eric anymore. He wasn't even a he, either.

A creature, hunched over and with tight, leathery skin, rose out of the tall, unkempt grass. Despite the brightness of the moon that shone above, the creature was shrouded in shadow.

The Nothing stood to its full height, and its shadowcloak fell to the ground.

There was a war in its mind, a war of understanding what had happened.

The Nothing that was no longer existed. There was only the Nothing that is, that stood in the backyard of the man whose body it had been absorbed into.

It had never taken a purely physical form before. It had previously thought it impossible.

In the moonlight, anyone who had known the Eric that was would have recognized his face even though it hid behind the mask of the Nothing. That man did what no one before him ever could and defeated the Nothing by giving custody of his full self to the anger that fought for control.

All of the smolder, all of the black water, all of the storm clouds were contained within the Nothing now. All of that had flowed into his *(NO)* its body and then the soul of the man ceased to exist.

There was only the Nothing now, and it was *hungry*.

It caught a scent on the wind and turned toward the east.

Hamilton, it knew from the knowledge the man used to have that it now possessed.

The Nothing broke into a run, or as much of a run as its awkward, limping gait would allow, blending into the shadows, heading toward where the sky was still bright

even at night.
    There, the Nothing knew with certainty.
    There was *plenty* to eat there.

(November 1, 2020 – December 4, 2020)

AUTHOR'S NOTE AND ACKNOWLEDGEMENTS

This story was inspired by a nightmare. Only a small part of this story came from what happened in that dream, but you'll have to guess as to which part.

Thank you to my wife Jessica, who was the first to read this story, and for offering your insights and edits on the first draft, and every draft thereafter.

To Mona, my editor, thank you for your keen eye and refinement. Please blame me for any remaining typos or errors you may find. To my beta readers and the people who were part of my launch team, thank you for your time, enthusiasm, and for helping this indie author get his book in the hands of others.

To the amazing community of horror readers and writers I've met and interacted with on Instagram, thank you for your support and help with launching this novella.

And now to you, Dear Reader.

I hope you enjoyed reading this book as much as I enjoyed writing it. If you did enjoy it, I ask that you please consider leaving a review on Amazon and/or Goodreads. For independent authors such as myself, reviews from readers help improve each book's ranking and visibility, which in turn helps out the author.

Thank you for taking a chance on my book.

Oh, and don't go walking in the woods at night. Dark things live in the shadows.

MRG

www.michaelrgoodwin.com

Michael is the author of the horror novel THE LIBERTY KEY, and a collection of short stories titled ROADSIDE FORGOTTEN.

He lives in Maine with his wife Jessica, their four children, and a variety of household pets.

For more information about the author or his upcoming projects, visit his website:

www.michaelrgoodwin.com

Lightning Source UK Ltd.
Milton Keynes UK
UKHW011214140421
381978UK00001B/111